Third Time's the Charm

Christian Cowboy Romance and Family Saga

Three Rivers Ranch Romance™
Book 2

Liz Isaacson

ISBN-13: 978-1-63876-322-2

"Be still, and know that I am God: I will be exalted among the heathen, I will be exalted in the earth."

Psalms 46:10

Chapter One

The strip of skin on Chelsea Ackerman's ring finger hadn't been so blindingly white before. Of course, the first time she'd been engaged, it had been winter. The second time had been during the previous two months when the Texas sun had been at its pinnacle. This past summer's heat alone could've bronzed her skin while she worked indoors—all except what the diamond had protected.

She stared at that line, taking her attention from the two-lane highway leading her home. Home to a ranch she didn't want. Home to an empty homestead now that her parents were moving into town. Home after her brother and his fiancée had left for College Station so he could finish his veterinarian degree.

A blaring horn caused her to jerk the steering wheel to the right. Since she'd drifted across the middle line, she didn't hit the gravelly shoulder on her side of the road. She skidded to a stop anyway, her pulse bobbing in the back of her throat.

The truck that roared past belonged to Three Rivers, but Chelsea didn't recognize the man who drove it. No surprise there. She hadn't been home since last Christmas, and she certainly didn't keep up with the personnel on her family's cattle ranch.

She glared at the taillights retreating in her rearview mirror, switching her laser-gaze back to the traitorous tan line on her left ring finger. Strong emotion welled where her lungs were, making it impossible to breathe.

Sucking at the air, she fumbled for the door handle, getting a blast of October heat when she spilled from her luxury SUV. She bent over and braced her elbows on her knees, still trying to get enough air, still trying to forget about the circumstances that had led her to this stretch of road in the Texas Panhandle.

As her lungs remembered how to work, she vowed she'd never wear another engagement ring.

Fool me once, shame on you. Fool me twice, shame on me.

There would not be a third time.

Chelsea collected herself, grateful for once for the low population of Three Rivers. She gathered her designer sunglasses from where they'd fallen on the asphalt and returned to the driver's seat. The air-conditioned seats drove away the heat, and when she sealed herself back in the SUV, the air had re-oxygenated itself.

Gripping the steering wheel, she prepared to keep on toward her destination, much as she didn't want to. A sign several yards down the road caught her attention. She inched the car forward until she could read the faded letters.

Three Rivers Ranch, 5. Five more miles until she met the worst turn her life had taken in the past twenty-eight years.

Beneath the old sign hung a much newer one. One that hadn't been there ten months ago.

Courage Reins Therapeutic Riding. No mileage included. Chelsea puzzled through what the sign could mean. Was this therapeutic riding program at the ranch?

Surely not. Someone would've mentioned as much to her. After all, she was the one taking over the management of the homestead until Squire graduated. The thought of planting and weeding her mother's massive vegetable garden made Chelsea feel twenty pounds heavier.

She pressed on the accelerator and centered the car in the appropriate lane. She'd find out about this Courage Reins in another five miles.

AT THE TURNOFF to Three Rivers, she squinted through the dusky sky to see another sign—new, with the same words. *Courage Reins.*

Annoyance sang through her. If the ranch had a new program, she should know about it.

She dismissed the thought. She wasn't in charge of the entire ranch. Her father had made that clear. She was to maintain the homestead—the house and the yard. Tom Lovell was the general controller and he oversaw the cowhands. Her father had hired a new foreman to replace the one who had been stealing money from the ranch for the past five years.

Chelsea sifted through her memories to remember his name. Garth Ahlstrom. He'd been foreman for a cattle ranch in Montana before making the move south. She shouldn't care about what happened once the grass of the homestead turned to the dirt parking lot on the ranch.

She pulled into the driveway leading to the garage, a wash of homesickness hitting her like a cold bucket of water. Which made no sense. She *was* home. This time, for a lot longer than it took to bake a ham and open presents.

She parked the car, but her fingers wouldn't release their grip on the wheel.

"Come on, Chels," she coaxed herself. "Just go in. It's going to be fine."

Fine wasn't quite the word she'd been using on the six-hour drive from Dallas. *Fine* wasn't the word her boss had used when she'd told him she was quitting to babysit a piece of land and a house. *Fine* wasn't the word that came to Chelsea's mind when she got the call from the hospital informing her of her fiancée's "accident."

She pushed away memories and remembrances of her life in Dallas. She didn't have a life in Dallas. Not anymore.

Her open-toed sandals drank up dust as she made her way into the garage. Once there, she scaled the steps to the entrance to the house. She braced herself for the smell of her mother's cooking to hit her upon the opening of the door. Surely her mom had been baking all afternoon in anticipation of Chelsea's arrival.

Sure enough, when she cracked the door, the scent of whole wheat bread slammed into her nostrils, along with the mouth-watering smell of roasting meat. She slipped through the mudroom and loitered in the doorway that led to the kitchen.

The ease with which her mother moved with a knife in her hand only served to remind Chelsea that she'd burned her last microwave meal. She wasn't fit to take care of the homestead, and anyone with one eye knew it.

"Hey, Mom." Chelsea ignored the skittering in her chest and the way her feet had grown roots.

"Chelsea, honey." Her mom set down the knife and moved around the counter for a hug. Chelsea managed to uproot herself and cross the room. "How was the drive?"

"Good," Chelsea lied. "Long." Only because she'd

turned around twice, driven for a few miles back toward Dallas before forcing herself north again.

Boxes lined the wall behind the dining room table, which was likewise stacked with packed garment bags, suitcases, and dishware.

"Sorry about the mess," her mom said, returning to the zucchini squash on the cutting board. "But we'll be gone tomorrow, and this place will be yours." Her voice carried too much gravity, breaking at the end.

Chelsea looked away as her mother wept, her own tears pressing so close, so close, so close.

"I'll go look at my room," she said, holding her breath as she clicked across the kitchen tile. Once in the safety of the hall, she released the air, which shuddered on the way out.

She didn't understand why her parents were leaving a house they clearly loved. Squire wouldn't need it for four more years. Chelsea certainly didn't need it now. She could've gone anywhere after the phone call that led to a hospital that led to her wearing black and speaking about Danny like he was the greatest man who'd lived.

A sob shook her shoulders, also knocking something loose inside her chest. Something that felt like her ability to sympathize, forgive, love.

Her mascara smeared when she wiped her eyes, but she didn't care. She wouldn't come out of her room tonight, not even for her mother's goodbye feast.

She didn't go down the hall to her old bedroom.

Instead, she slipped downstairs and outside to the patio sheltered by a deck above. She perched on a decorative boulder and let the darkness inside her spread until even her tears felt like tar leaking from her eyes.

"You okay, ma'am?"

Chelsea startled at the masculine tone, wiping again at her face. Her fingers came away stained with black and blue. So much for waterproof makeup.

"I'm fine." She didn't mean for her voice to blow through the space like an arctic wind. She turned toward the man and found a tall specimen with more muscles than she knew could be contained by skin.

The concern in his green eyes frosted at her tone, and as he crossed his arms, Chelsea saw the puckered and pink skin of a burn on his right side. The mark extended under the sleeves of the blue T-shirt he wore and marred all the fingers on his right hand.

"Of course you are," he said. "I regularly cry in a remote place on the ranch because I'm *fine*."

She didn't need this stranger judging her, and she certainly wasn't in the mood for company.

"It's none of your concern." She stood like she'd march away, but realized she didn't have anywhere else to go. Though she wasn't happy to be here, she didn't want to make things harder for her mother.

He saluted her. "If you say so." He ambled to the stone steps he must've come down. She hadn't heard him in her distress.

Her breath hitched and the writhing in her stomach felt like she'd swallowed snakes.

He was leaving, the same way Danny had left.

"What do you do on the ranch?" she called after him, suddenly desperate to keep him there for a few more minutes.

The man twisted back to her but maintained his position on the steps. "I'm opening the new therapeutic riding program."

And she wanted him to leave again. "Courage Reins. I saw the signs on the way in." She reseated herself and flicked an imaginary piece of lint from her leggings. "What is it?"

His gaze gave none of his emotions away. "It's a therapeutic riding program." He spoke slower, like perhaps she didn't understand English.

"What—does—it—do?" She dragged out each word in case his hearing had been affected in whatever accident had given him that burn.

"We take individuals who've been through trauma, and we help them with their rehabilitation."

"So like physical therapy."

"Any kind of trauma," he said.

She swept her gaze meaningfully toward his arm. "Like yours."

His gaze bored into hers, straight past every one of her defenses. "Or yours." He turned and marched up the steps, leaving Chelsea gasping for breath and grasping for something to keep her from drowning under the sudden memories of Danny's death.

Dear Lord, she prayed. *Help me.*

In her distress, she couldn't articulate much more than that.

* * *

Pete Marshall stalked away from Squire's sister, the scarred skin covered by his shirt prickling uncomfortably. The princess obviously thought all wounds were physical. Pete knew better, had overheard the Ackerman's say something about their daughter's boyfriend at breakfast a while back.

He'd been so absorbed with getting Courage Reins off the ground, he hadn't paid as much attention as he might have otherwise. All he knew was that she'd quit her job and volunteered to return to Three Rivers so her parents could move into town.

Pete already missed Frank and Heidi and they weren't moving until tomorrow. All their cowhands were helping, Pete included.

He paused outside the horse barn, regret singing through him. He wasn't just opening Courage Reins—he worked the ranch too. And Chelsea was obviously in distress, and she didn't need him exacerbating her condition. He turned around to go back to the house, hoping she'd still be weeping on the downstairs patio. Well, maybe not the crying bit. He had no idea how to deal with weepy women.

The sight of her stomping toward him froze him to the path. Her chestnut brown hair swung in time to her hips as her sandals ate up the distance between them.

"Look," she called from several yards away. "I don't know who you think you are, but I'm going to be taking over the homestead."

"I know, sweetheart."

She stopped a few feet away, flinching as if the lash of his endearment had struck like a backhand to her cheek.

"Who are you?"

"First Lieutenant Peter Marshall." He saluted again, sure she didn't want him touching her if the crossed arms and cocked hip were any indication. Pete had certain skills when it came to reading people, and Chelsea screamed *angry*.

The creases around her eyes softened. "Did you serve with my brother?"

"Twice."

Her eyes flickered to his scars again, and Pete worked hard to keep his expression neutral and the flush down in his chest where she couldn't see it. His injuries belonged to him now, no matter how much he wished they didn't. He'd had a year to get used to the idea, and the past few months of attending church with the Ackerman's had helped him accept God's will.

He was still here, after all. Still alive. And with the

concept of Courage Reins getting off the ground, Pete finally felt like he had a *reason* to be here, a purpose for being alive.

"I'm sorry," he said into the gusting silence between them. "I shouldn't have snapped at you back there, what with you crying and all."

"I said I was—"

"Fine, I know." The sun made an appearance behind the evening clouds. He pushed his cowboy hat lower over his eyes. "You want to go riding anyway? It makes some people feel better."

"I feel fine."

Sure she did. Pete had told himself that for months too, but he also knew she needed time for her own grieving. "Suit yourself. I have a client tomorrow evening, after your parents move, so I need to do a test ride." He hooked his thumb over his shoulder toward the horse barn. "Last chance."

The color drained from Chelsea's face, but it could've been a trick of the fading light. She shook her head, spun on her heel, and hurried away from him like he had a contagious disease.

He saddled Peony and headed along the path he'd mapped out. Past the horse pasture, the bull pens, and out onto the range. His hope was that by bringing people to the ranch they'd find the same comfort, the same peace, the same rehabilitation he'd felt in his body and soul when he'd come to Three Rivers.

The sky turned the color of a deep bruise, and he directed Peony back to the barn. The man coming tomorrow afternoon had suffered some core injuries during his deployment. Working with a horse could provide a bond that would help his self-confidence, and once he learned to ride, he'd be able to work his core muscles as he balanced and directed the horse.

Pete had decided to have Reese start with Peony in the barn first. Brushing, saddling. Then he'd lead her around the arena before Pete would allow him to ride. He had a game of pony ball ready if the veteran could handle it.

The package he'd sold included six weekly sessions of two hours each, and as Pete brushed Peony he let his mind wander to future packages and how he could get the word out about the program to other veterans. Without many new ideas, he closed up the barn for the night and returned to the cabin where he lived alone now that Squire had moved to College Station with his fiancée, Kelly Armstrong.

He flipped open his laptop and searched for information on therapeutic programs for veterans. It wasn't the first time he'd researched other facilities, but just as with the previous few times, the amount of information available became overwhelming after only five minutes.

Pete reached for a pen and scratched out a few more notes to himself. *Research how to join PATH International* and *ask Squire about purchasing land for the facility* got added to his list before he headed over to the homestead for Heidi and Frank's farewell dinner.

As he walked, Chelsea's haunted midnight blue eyes filled his mind. The woman needed help, and as Pete entered the halo of light radiating from the kitchen, he felt certain God wanted him to aid in her rehabilitation.

Chapter Two

Chelsea was unsuccessful in her attempts to avoid her parents. The lighter knock of her father was followed by the no-nonsense rap of her mother. "Chelsea," she called through the wood. "I am not letting you shut yourself off in there."

Chelsea padded across her old bedroom to the door and cracked it. She'd tucked her legs under her body on the bed by the time her mom entered. She swept her gaze over Chelsea, who had changed into a loose pair of yoga pants and one of Danny's old shirts, a gray Cowboys tee.

"Honey." Her mom's love filled the room and she gathered Chelsea into her arms. Though Chelsea felt like she was shaking the earth and shattering from the inside out, her mother didn't let go.

Several minutes passed, until the storm inside Chelsea had raged out. "I'm okay." Her voice sounded as thick as brownie batter. It had been months since Danny's death. She should be okay.

"You're not okay," her mom said. "And that's okay. You don't need to be okay right now. In fact, if you were okay right now, I would be worried." She took Chelsea's face in her hands, and Chelsea wondered if she'd ever be as strong as her mom. Her eyes shone with the iron she possessed and the solid line of her mouth spoke of it.

"We can stay as long as you need."

Chelsea shook her head before her mom stopped speaking. "No," she said. "I would've left Dallas no matter what." She could've gone anywhere, and truthfully the thought of driving forty minutes to the grocery store brought a twist to her stomach that told Chelsea she'd rather starve than face the townspeople.

"I know the ranch wasn't your first choice."

Chelsea wished she could reassure her mom with more than, "It's going to be fine." She heard Pete's voice when she said the last word, and she couldn't help remembering the emerald blaze in his eyes when he challenged her to come riding with him.

She hadn't told anyone that Danny wasn't well, and she'd be taking that knowledge to the grave. She'd loved him, but that hadn't been enough. She didn't want to mother him, and every time they disagreed and he slumped into his depression, she blamed herself.

Her tears weren't for what she'd lost when Danny had ended his life. They were because she was beyond relieved to be free from him, his moods that held her hostage, his anxiety that caged her when he didn't feel like socializing, or working, or getting off the couch.

No one could ever know her tears came from a place of relief. What kind of monster did that make her?

She straightened her shoulders and strengthened herself with a stuttering breath. "Let's go eat. The beef smells delicious."

"Home grown." Her mom smiled as she linked her elbow through Chelsea's and moved with her out of the bedroom and down the hall.

Her father sat at the kitchen table with Pete Marshall. Chelsea's withered heart pumped out an extra beat, which caused her lips to sink. Her stupid body must not have gotten the message that she was out of the dating game for good.

"Hello," she said as pleasantly as she could manage. At least her voice didn't sound like a teenage boy going through puberty.

"Evenin', ma'am." He removed his hat to show off his sandy blond hair. Chelsea had always found it fascinating how a man could remove his cowboy hat and become a completely different person.

"Heidi, this smells like the best meal you've ever made."

"Oh, go on." Her mother blushed at Pete's compliment. They joined hands, and Chelsea hoped comfort and strength could be gathered through osmosis as her father said grace. As her parents and Pete tucked into the roast and mashed potatoes, Chelsea found herself watching Pete. Since when did the cowhands eat with her family? Maybe those who'd served with Squire got special treatment.

Chelsea followed the conversation but didn't participate. Just like she'd been doing for the last couple of months. Living, breathing, watching. But not participating.

By the time dishes started clacking, signaling the end of the meal, Chelsea had succeeded in swallowing a couple of bites of food. She cleared her plate with everyone else, hoping no one would say anything.

Her mother saw the mashed potatoes Chelsea scraped into the sink, but she kept quiet. Chelsea focused on the dishes, soaping and rinsing in a methodical way. Anything to keep her mind from wandering.

By the time she looked up, only Pete remained in the kitchen. He leaned casually against the counter, watching her with those intense eyes. So open. So unassuming.

"I've been helpin' around the homestead," he said. "Minor construction repairs, painting, that kind of thing. Your dad's been so busy getting Garth up to speed, and your mom wanted everything perfect for when you arrived."

Chelsea seemed to have swallowed her ability to speak. So she nodded until she could say, "Thank you, Pete."

"If there's anything you need after they move out, don't hesitate to ask."

"Sure, of course."

Pete tipped his hat in farewell and stepped out the French doors to the deck. She watched him until the night swallowed him, wishing she was brave enough to ask him to paint the bathroom and retile the mudroom. But she knew she wouldn't. Spending too much time with anyone would require her to talk, and she certainly didn't want that.

* * *

Twenty-four hours later, Chelsea rose from her parent's new dining room table. Boxes gaped open from when she and her mom had searched through them for silverware and cups. They'd eaten leftovers and set up the kitchen and bedrooms enough to function until her parents could unpack the rest of their belongings.

"Well, I better head back."

Her dad drew her into a hug, and it almost erased the last year of her life. Almost. For the first few months in their relationship, Chelsea thought she could be the light Danny needed. He seemed to function better once they'd started dating. She could get him to go out to dinner if they went somewhere unpopular, away from the crowds. He held his position with the postal service longer than he had any other job.

When he'd asked her to marry him, she hadn't seen the worst of his depression yet.

Her pulse surged up her throat at those memories, and she worked to shove them back where they belonged—in her past.

"Drive carefully, baby," her dad said.

Chelsea hugged her mom and promised to come help unpack in the morning. Her headlights cut a path through the darkness that made seeing the stars magnificent. Without anyone else on the road, Chelsea aimed her SUV right down the middle of the highway and switched on the radio.

The soothing sound of classical music lilted through the speakers. She hadn't listened to her beloved string quartets since Danny told her music without words unsettled him. She'd rearranged entire aspects of her life to try to make him happy. Nothing had worked.

She pulled into the driveway, glad her parents had motion-sensor lighting. She dropped her purse in the mudroom and kicked off her running shoes, sighing as she leaned against the closed door.

The three thousand square foot house loomed around her, a massive physical presence that pressed on her shoulders. She had a TV in her old bedroom, so she didn't need the living room upstairs. Or the one downstairs.

Tomorrow, she'd help her mother unpack in the morning and in the afternoon, she'd begin closing off some of the rooms that wouldn't be used over the next four years.

Upon rounding the corner into the kitchen, the flickering light of the TV caught her attention. She couldn't hear the volume, or anyone else in the house. But she hadn't left the television on.

She crossed the eat-in dining room, noting the absolute blackness outside the huge windows that looked over the yard and toward the ranch.

"Hello?" She could barely hear herself, especially over the drumming of her heart.

Nothing stirred, though the closer she crept, the clearer the steady breathing of a body became. She peeked over the edge of the couch and found Pete asleep, his handsome face more youthful while so relaxed.

The adrenaline that had invaded her body drained away. What was he doing here? As a cowhand, he probably lived in one of the cabins, but she didn't think she'd be seeing him in the house once her parents moved out.

She allowed herself to examine his burnt arm longer than was proper when one was awake. From fingertip to sleeve, sweeping from the outside of his arm in, a blanket of pink, wavy scar tissue stood out angrily against his sun-kissed skin. She wanted to know the story behind his injury and how it had affected him psychologically. He didn't seem as broken as she was.

She had the urge to run her fingers over his, maybe to smooth out the wrinkles.

Stop it, she commanded herself. *You cannot fix him.*

She spun away, the little she'd eaten at dinner threatening to reappear. She took several steps and braced herself against the kitchen counter, sucking and sucking for oxygen. She felt like a fish, like air was the wrong thing to breathe.

High-pitched noise escaped her throat, fading into the tornado that had started bellowing in her ears.

"Hey." A deep voice sounded as if in a tunnel. A heavy, heated weight landed on the middle of her back. "It's okay. Breathe deep. Just one breath. With me. Ready?"

The heat spread in a circle as he rubbed her back.

"You didn't breathe, Chelsea."

She was able to identify the voice as Pete's.

"Come on now, sweetheart." His hand slipped around her shoulder and he pulled her into his chest. "Breathe in with me. One, two, three." His chest inflated, and she forced hers to go with it.

"Hold there," he whispered.

The scent of his skin, musky and clean, penetrated her panic.

"And out." He released his breath, and she followed suit, her control returning inch by inch.

She came to her senses and released the tightness in her fingers, which were clenched in his shirt against his chest. "I'm sorry." But she didn't move, safe as she felt in the circle of his arms.

"Can you walk? You want to sit down?"

She realized he supported her full weight with his hands anchored around her waist. She found her footing, a new sort of thrumming vibrating her ribs. She let him guide her to the couch, where she sat on the edge, the house too cold without Pete's embrace.

"Sorry," she said again.

"How long have you been having panic attacks?" He sat next to her, close enough to reach out and touch if she needed the anchor.

"I don't—I mean—"

"I had them for six months after my tank got bombed." He spoke with reverence, and Chelsea had enough awareness to notice his eyes took on a faraway quality. "Now it's just the dreams that haunt me."

"You have nightmares?"

"Not since I started trying to get this therapeutic thing off the ground." He yawned. "Too tired. Sorry I fell asleep waitin' for you. Your mom called. Wanted me to make sure you got here safely."

Safely was a relative term. Physically, she'd made it. Emotionally, she was knotted and pretzeled and snarled with remorse and relief and guilt and guilt and guilt.

"Thank you," ghosted between her lips.

"Like I said earlier, anytime." He met her gaze, and he looked made of steel. She remembered the sturdiness of his arms, his chest. She swallowed and wiped the back of her hand against her forehead.

"I think I better get to bed."

He stood with her, but a slithery feeling still soured Chelsea's stomach. She sank back to the couch. "Maybe I'll just sleep here." Her voice sounded wispy, like cobwebs and dust. "You made it look pretty comfortable."

Pete retrieved a blanket from the opposite end of the couch and covered her with it. "You have a cell phone?"

She nodded, her vocal cords done for the day.

"Chelsea?" His handsome face appeared inches from hers. "Where is it, sweetheart? I'll put my number in it in case you need anything."

"My purse." Her eyes drifted closed as his sure footsteps crossed the kitchen to find her purse. She didn't know if he found it. She didn't know if he stayed. She didn't know if she'd survive alone in this house.

Pete, now wide-awake after his catnap, sat as far from Chelsea as he could while staying on the couch. The TV droned in the background, but he kept his attention on the waif of a woman across from him.

Though she probably wanted to be left alone, he couldn't do it. He watched her chest rise and fall, rise and fall, as the minutes ticked closer to midnight. He'd be hurting in the morning, but right now, a woman's life was more important.

A beautiful woman, he thought before he could censor himself.

Though Chelsea possessed the dark hair and bright eyes he was normally attracted to, he didn't need the obvious baggage she brought with her. Pete had enough of his own.

He had seen steel in her expression on more than one occasion. When she tromped through the dust to chew him out. When she ate dinner with her parents like everything was normal. When she hauled box after box to the moving van.

She fell into a deep sleep, and Pete rose to find her bedroom. Down the hall and up a short series of steps, he found what had probably been Squire's old digs. The cricket posters were a dead giveaway. Pete couldn't help smiling as he thought about his Army friend.

A squeeze against his heart reminded Pete of how much he owed Major Ackerman. This job. His life.

Around the corner sat another bedroom, this one obviously Chelsea's, what with the flowered bedspread and lilac walls. It didn't speak of a little girl though, but a sophisticated woman. He stepped inside, touching his fingers to the top of her dresser, where she'd laid her jewelry and a notebook.

He turned down the covers before returning to the living room. He scooped her into his arms with little effort and carried her down the hall. She didn't moan or move or make any indication other than breathing that she was alive.

Pete felt her sadness simply by holding her. He knew she wasn't eating enough by the way her jeans bagged and how skeletal she felt against him. He placed her in bed and smoothed her hair off her forehead.

"I can help you," he whispered. "Or rather, the horses can." He straightened and drank her in one last time before heading to his cabin. He wasn't going to give up on Chelsea. He'd get her to participate in his therapeutic riding program, no matter the cost.

* * *

THE NEXT MORNING, Pete had four horses brushed down before anyone else showed up on the ranch.

"What's his name?"

He turned toward the soft voice coming from behind him. Chelsea stood there, wearing a different pair of jeans and a sweatshirt, though the October weather certainly wasn't cold.

"This is Peony," he said, motioning Chelsea forward. She joined him at the rail, her hands hidden in her pockets.

"I'm training her for my riding program."

She stiffened, almost imperceptibly, but Pete noticed. Peony swung her dark eyes toward Chelsea and lifted her nose above the rail. Chelsea stepped back, alarm coloring her face.

"How'd your lesson go last night?"

"Good," Pete said. "I'm just getting started. Training the horses, and myself, and figuring out what to do with the patients." He exhaled, the sound revealing more than he liked. "I'm sort of flying blind right now."

"What do you mean?" Chelsea stepped up to Peony, tentatively stroking her hands down the horse's cheeks.

"Well...." Pete slid her a sideways glance and found her expression open and unassuming.

"I need money." He leaned his elbows against the rail as Baywatch ambled over. "I need facilities exclusively for the program. I need a therapist, and grants, and volunteers, and there's this veteran's program called PATH International I need to join, and—" He forced himself to shut his mouth. It had taken him a couple of months to absorb all the information on starting and running an equine therapeutic riding program. Surely he sounded like he was speaking another language.

"It sounds like you know what you're doing."

He detected a smile in her voice. "I have no clue," he admitted. "Reese is an old Army pal. He doesn't mind that I'm experimenting on him, but after last night, I know a little bit about what I'm lacking."

She placed her hand on his arm, drawing his attention from the horses to her fingers. Long and slender, they sent a chill through his skin. She shouldn't be this cold. She drew back, and Pete followed the movement before meeting her gaze.

She swallowed, shuttering her emotions behind a false grin. "I'm sure you'll figure it out."

Challenge rose through Pete. "You don't even know me. How do you know I can do this?"

"I made breakfast this morning without burning down the house," she said. "If I can do that, you can do this."

"Starting a non-profit organization that needs a staff and dozens of volunteers is a lot harder than pouring a bowl of cereal, sweetheart." He stalked away from the horses, his frustration reaching a level he couldn't contain.

Her footfalls followed his. "Listen," she called behind him. "It was a lot more than cereal."

"Oh yeah? Protein shake?"

"I *cooked*," she said, a point she enunciated so vehemently that Pete realized its significance.

He paused just outside the barn's entrance, the morning sun brightening his mood. "Okay," he said. "Want to make me breakfast?"

"Absolutely not." She folded her arms and seemed to deflate in the sunlight. "I don't need to embarrass myself any more than I already have."

Pete noticed the determined set of her jaw. "You haven't embarrassed yourself."

"No?" Her eyebrows disappeared under her bangs. "So having a panic attack and then conking out is normal in your world?"

"Pretty normal, yeah." He took a deep breath and caught the creamy scent of her skin or her shampoo. He wanted to breathe her in all day, so he purposefully took a step away. "Having anxiety after experiencing a traumatic event is nothing to be ashamed of."

"Who says I've experienced a traumatic event?"

Pete peered at her, uncertain of how to proceed. "No one," he decided to say. "I have an idea, though...."

He didn't think her hip could cock any further, but it did. "Oh?"

"How about you let me experiment on you, too?" He rushed to add, "With the horses? Not that *you* need therapy, but to train them?"

"I don't think so." She started back toward the homestead.

"Why not?" He hurried to follow her. "Surely you already know how to ride a horse."

"Of course I do," she said. "It's just been a long time."

"Even better," he said. "I need the horses to behave a certain way with anyone, regardless of their experience or lack thereof."

"Lack thereof?" She stopped on the edge of the yard. "Where'd you come from?"

He smelled a victory, if only he pushed a little further. "Tennessee," he said. "Bachelor's in business management." His desperation clogged his throat. "Please. I need riders to train the horses, and I know I can make this program a success."

He had no idea how, but kernels incubated in his mind. Nothing would matter if he didn't have the right horses for his equine program.

"Once a week," he pushed. "A couple of hours, once a week."

"I'll consult my schedule." Chelsea gave him a curt nod goodbye before she made her way across the lawn to the deck. Pete watched her go, the scent of victory almost as sweet as her perfume.

Chapter Three

The house still smelled like fried, fried, *fried* eggs, a scent that brought a twist to Chelsea's stomach. It definitely wasn't because of the little fib she'd told Pete. She had made breakfast, she'd definitely cooked, and she hadn't burned down the house.

He'd never asked if the food was edible. She pulled the bag containing that morning's failure out of the trashcan and took it out to the barrel. Back inside, she located a can of disinfectant spray and applied a generous dose to the kitchen, empty dining room, and living room.

She collapsed on the couch where she'd fallen asleep last night, unsure of what to do next. She'd woken before dawn and spent a couple of hours before her egg disaster closing up the basement.

Her parents had taken the smaller sofa and love seat from the basement for their smaller house in town. They'd left the huge sectional upstairs, half their towel collection, a couple of barstools for the kitchen, and all the patio furniture.

Since Chelsea was a party of one, she didn't need a dining room table, but the space gaped now that it didn't house anything. Only halfway to lunch on the first day at the homestead, and already Chelsea was wondering what she would do all day, everyday.

She heaved herself to her feet and located her phone. After sending a text to her mother that she'd come help unpack later, her thoughts returned to Pete. She'd gone to the barn that morning to thank him for his kindness, for helping her last night. Embarrassment threaded through her when she thought of him carrying her to bed, but she felt braver now than she had in person.

Thanks for helping me last night, she typed. Her thumb hovered over the send button as she read and reread her message. It was a simple expression of gratitude. He deserved it.

But his words looped in her mind. *Having anxiety after experiencing a traumatic event is nothing to be ashamed of.*

Her anxiety had grown each day since Danny's death. She couldn't deny that and wasn't sure she wanted to.

It was the traumatic experience she was unsure of. She hadn't been there when Danny died. She hadn't even been allowed to see him in the hospital. The funeral had been carried out with a closed casket. That was what happened when someone used a firearm in close quarters.

She hadn't returned to Danny's apartment. His parents had identified the body. She hadn't *seen* anything, except what her imagination could conjure up in quiet moments.

Was that a traumatic experience?

Chelsea didn't think so. She didn't have burns like Pete, or missing limbs, or a limp like her brother. She hadn't even been present during the event.

Maybe that was why everything inside her mind no longer made sense. Real thoughts took so much time to tunnel to the surface, and even longer for her to mull over before she spoke them.

She didn't need to speak to take an inventory of the gardening equipment. She noted that the lawn had just been clipped, the flower beds weeded, and most of the garden cleared except for the squashes that still spread their vines across the ground. She'd need to get the yard ready for the winter, though, and she needed to know what tools she had at her disposal.

After a sweaty hour in the shed, she returned to the house for a shower. By the time she emerged from the hot water, her stomach growled for lunch. Since she'd attempted cooking for breakfast, she decided to forgo anything to do with the stove and stuck a container of soup in the microwave.

She paired it with a piece of toast, but only ate four

bites before she couldn't get another spoonful of stew past her lips.

A knock on the patio doors sent her heart rippling, and she twisted from her place on a barstool to see Pete enter the kitchen.

"Lunch," he said. "Smells good."

"My mom said I didn't have to feed the cowhands." It had been the one thing Chelsea had insisted on.

"I know," he said, stepping to the fridge and opening it. He had to stoop to look inside, a crease forming between his emerald eyes. "Oh, I forgot your mom took all the good stuff." He let the door swing closed before he leaned against the refrigerator.

"I have yogurt and cottage cheese in there," Chelsea said.

"Chick food." His mouth twitched with a smirk. "It's okay. I have bread and turkey in my cabin."

She spread her hands around her soup bowl. If she couldn't eat it, she could use the warmth to try to heat her fingers. Since Danny's death, she hadn't been able to stay warm, almost like her body had forgotten it wasn't reptilian.

"Then why are you here?" she asked.

His jaw hardened. "Just saying hello."

Right. She resisted the urge to call him on his obvious lie. He had no reason to come to the house.

"Are you checking up on me?"

"Are you suggesting you need to be checked up on?"

He folded his arms, which was much more impressive than when she did. He increased his presence while she seemed to fold into herself.

"No," she said. "But I wouldn't put it past my mother to be asking you for a daily report."

He laughed, the noise joyful and happy and wonderful. Everything Chelsea wasn't. She wanted to bottle the sound and listen to it whenever she needed to smile.

"Your mother should get a daily report," Pete said. "But not from me."

"I'm not going to call my mother every day."

"You should."

"Why?" And why did he care?

"She's concerned about you, that's why." Pete pushed off the fridge. "It wouldn't kill you to text her and let her know you're okay. Tell her about your cooking success this morning. That kind of thing."

"Do you text your mother?"

"I would if she was still alive."

Chelsea's heart burned like a live coal, creating a hole in her chest. He'd experienced loss, like she had. "I'm so sorry." She spoke so softly, he leaned forward to catch the words.

"I was in Afghanistan when she died in a car accident with my granddad." The muscles in his neck tightened though his tone stayed even. "I missed their funerals, but I stopped by their graves in Tennessee before I came out here."

Tears filled her eyes, just like they had during Danny's service. The scratchiness of lace along her collar made her lift her fingers to her neck, just as she had during Danny's service. The scent of orange and cloying rose petals filled her nose, just as they had during Danny's service.

She blinked, and Pete's fair features turned dark. Dark hair. Dark, enthralling eyes that sparkled when Danny played the guitar and sang. Deep, brooding eyes that begged her for help.

Once, she'd thought she could help him. That by loving him enough, he wouldn't need anything else.

How wrong she'd been.

"Hey, it's okay." Pete stepped closer to her. "It's been a few years."

Her chin shook as she swiped at her eyes. "Does time make it easier?" Surprise shot through her at her own boldness. She hadn't meant to ask, didn't even know she had the question inside.

Pete's eyes became like pools. Pools of warm liquid Chelsea could lose herself in, swim in for hours and still not be satisfied.

"Yes," he whispered. "It does." His arm moved, his fingers touching hers for a quick moment. So quick she wasn't sure he'd actually made contact. "Time, and distance, and finding another purpose."

She thought of his therapeutic riding program, the heaviness in his voice when he spoke about what he needed to get it started, his invitation to help train the horses.

"I can help with the horses." Chelsea lifted her chin a couple of inches to look into his eyes.

He gazed down on her, but she didn't feel small or weak. "Tonight?"

"Sure, why not?"

"I'll come get you after dinner." He stepped past her and headed outside.

As she watched him descend the steps and cross the lawn, she thought, *Why not indeed?*

* * *

THE NEXT SEVERAL hours dragged for Pete as he fed horses and rode out to the hay barn to check the supply for the oncoming winter. All he could think about was his program, how he could benefit both Chelsea and Peony during the session that evening.

Just before dinner, he called Squire, hoping he was out of class or work or whatever he was doing in College Station.

"Hey," the Major said. "How's the ranch?"

"Good, fine," Pete answered, his words suddenly stuck behind a lump in his throat.

"So what's going on?" Squire never was one to mince words.

"Your sister made it home."

"Good," Squire said. "How is she?"

"She's in bad shape, Major. I don't know everything that happened, or why she really came home, but she's not okay."

Squire exhaled as the silence lengthened. "What happened?"

"She had a panic attack last night."

"Do you know why?"

"Didn't ask. Just tried to help her through it."

This silence didn't feel as safe as the previous one. "What do you mean by 'help her through it'?"

"Taught her how to breathe. I have some other tricks up my sleeve, which leads me to why I'm calling."

"Oh?"

"Remember me talking about an equine therapeutic riding program?"

"Yeah, you started training Peony before I left."

"Right, she's done a session or two. I'm training Baywatch too, and Chelsea's agreed to help me with the horses. But I need grants, and volunteers, and facilities to really have a true program." He stopped talking, though his thoughts raced like thoroughbreds.

"Facilities?"

"Here's what I'm thinking. I get a loan to purchase part of the ranch. A dozen or so acres, for the facilities I need. You know, a riding track and a dedicated arena to work with the horses, a small office building. If you'll let me use the barn and your retired horses, we can be partners. Three Rivers Ranch and Courage Reins."

This silence sounded deafening, like the stretch of soundlessness that had poured through Pete's ears just after the bomb hit the tank. Then the pain had registered. The screaming. The smoke.

He inhaled deliberately, calming the rough edges inside his chest with mere oxygen.

"I'm sure Three Rivers can spare a dozen acres," Squire said. "Sounds like this program has really gotten under your skin, Lieutenant."

"Yeah," Pete said, unwilling for the moment to elaborate. Courage Reins wasn't just under his skin. It had become his passion, something he contemplated every waking moment of his life. "I'll meet with the bank next week."

"Which horses you usin' besides Peony and Baywatch?"

"I think I'll need at least a couple more—maybe Juniper and Hank?—and maybe another couple once the program expands. But that won't be for a while." He added the last part in a rush so Squire wouldn't think Pete was taking every able-bodied horse available.

"Sounds good," he said. "How's Juniper?"

Pete detected a trace of emotion in the Major's tone. "She's doin' fine. I think I'm going to ride her tonight while Chelsea trains with Peony."

"Sounds good." Squire paused and Pete listened to the

silence to predict what he might say next. "You take good care of my sister, Lieutenant. She needs it."

"Of course." Pete pressed his mouth closed. It wasn't his place to tell Squire how much help his sister really needed.

* * *

PETE SMELLED the smoke from inside the barn. He broke into a sprint as he crossed the lawn and took the stairs to the deck two at a time. He yanked open the door. "Chelsea?"

"I'm fine!" she called from somewhere amid the smoke. Someone really needed to teach this woman the definition of *fine*.

He pulled his shirt over his mouth and left the door open. He maneuvered to the counter, one arm in front of him sweeping for obstacles. His heart drummed against the roof of his mouth, pounding, searching, beating, scanning.

A towel whipped his arm, and he seized it. Chelsea came with it and he tucked her against his side and moved toward the exit. "What happened?"

"I tried cooking again." A cough rattled her body as Pete helped her to the deck and turned back to the house. He re-entered, taking a few seconds to open all the windows on the east wall. Tom's voice reached him through the haze.

"Over here," Pete called, moving around the counter to the stove, where several pancake shaped hockey pucks smoldered. She'd managed to turn off the burners, but the griddle radiated heat a good six inches above its surface.

"There's an extinguisher under the sink," Tom said, his outline appearing through the smoke.

"I think it just needs to air out. Can't see a flame." Pete used the spatula and removed the offending pancakes. He tossed them into the sink and ran water over them.

"That thing is screamin' hot," he said as Tom stepped toward the stove. "Can we put water on it?"

"That'll just steam some more," Tom said. "Let's just let it cool off."

"I think my mother has a fan in the shed," Chelsea said from Pete's right. "I'll go get it."

Pete didn't need to be breathing smoke so he followed Tom onto the deck, where twilight sucked up the mist and dispersed it.

"We'll never get another home cooked meal," Tom said.

Pete watched Chelsea cross the yard, her back straight and her steps sure. "No, probably not."

Tom grumbled as he descended the steps. Pete waited for Chelsea to return, and he took the fan, setting it next to the stove and blowing the smoke toward the doors and windows.

"Let's go get something to eat at my cabin," he said,

hooking his arm through Chelsea's and towing her toward the steps.

"I'm not hungry."

"Then why were you making pancakes?"

"Practicing."

Pete's heart squeezed, but he couldn't help laughing. "I'm sorry," he said, still chuckling. "But it looks like you need more practice."

She slipped her arm down so that her hand rested in the crook of his elbow. "Stop it. I don't have much to do, and I figured how hard could making pancakes be?"

"Right. Well, you didn't quite burn down the house."

"There's always tomorrow."

Pete groaned. "If you're going to be doing a lot of cooking, maybe I should be there to supervise." He glanced at her. "I mean, watch. *Encourage.*"

The stiff line around her mouth softened, and her enormous eyes swung his way, captivating him in an instant. His step stumbled as a spark of attraction sprang from her to him. He narrowed his eyes to break their connection, heat rising from deep within his core.

"So what do I need to do with the horses tonight?" she asked.

"Nothing specific," Pete said. "I want you to do whatever you do."

"But what if I spook them?"

"It's their job not to get spooked, sweetheart. I'm

training them to work with disabled veterans, or kids with Autism. They can handle you."

At least Pete hoped they could. Just because Chelsea hadn't seen active duty didn't mean she wasn't as emotionally scarred.

Chapter Four

Chelsea warred with herself as she and Pete approached the horse barn. She should let go of his arm, what with that electricity flowing between them so freely. But she needed the comfort and strength of his touch and couldn't force herself to release him.

Her nerves quivered like they'd been shredded by a lawn trimmer. The horses would be able to feel her tension, but she didn't know how to tame it. She hadn't been able to for weeks.

Months, she thought, if she were being honest. For the last few months of Danny's life, she'd lived as an emotional hostage. A slave to his mood, his needs. She'd found him selfish, but she'd reasoned that away under the umbrella of his depression.

"Chelsea?"

"Hmm?" She realized they'd stopped outside Peony's stall.

"I need my arm, sweetheart."

She let go of him as if he'd caught fire. Her face had certainly found the flame. "Sorry."

In his absence, she reached for the horse. Peony closed her eyes halfway, and Chelsea stroked her eggshell colored hair, a sigh softening her insides.

Pete opened the gate and entered the stall with a horse blanket and saddle. He equipped Peony and stepped out. "You're going to ride her."

Her organs seized again. "First thing?"

"If you don't want to, that's fine," he said. "You can lead her around the arena. Kick her a ball. Get comfortable with her."

Chelsea liked that idea better, though it made her feel like *she* was the one being trained.

"Isn't she getting comfortable with me?"

Peony pushed her nose into Chelsea's shoulder.

"I think she already is, sweetheart." Pete leaned against the rail. "But she needs to go through the activities I'll be using with the real patients. I can do it if you'd rather."

Her defenses rose at his suggestion. "No, I want to do it. Plus, you need to practice being the instructor, right?"

"Right." He straightened and moved into her personal bubble. "Ready?"

She gazed up at him, captivated by his presence, his

warmth. Her hands hurt from the constant cold. "Ready," misted from her mouth.

He stepped back and she almost fell forward. She followed him through the gate and took Peony's reins.

"Walk 'er back this way," Pete instructed from the back of the stall, where a barred hallway led to the outside arena. He lifted the bar and indicated for Chelsea to go first. "Go as slow as you want. We want Peony to obey your commands, go with you, basically submit to you."

"Come on, girl." Chelsea stepped and clicked her tongue the way she had as a child and Peony went with her.

Swells of pride filled her and filled her. "She's coming."

Pete's smile matched hers. "Take 'er all the way out. I'll meet you out there. Remember, it's never safe to walk behind a horse. They don't like it."

Chelsea placed her hand on his arm as she passed. A fleeting touch, but one that carried weight. What kind of weight, she wasn't sure. She just knew he made her feel.... He made her *feel*.

He waited in the arena when she and Peony exited the barn. "Take 'er around the outside," he instructed. "Just get a feel for her."

Chelsea matched her footsteps with the plodding of the horse's hooves. Her heartbeat found the rhythm too, and though it was dark beyond the lit arena, Chelsea didn't feel any of it inside herself.

"Talk to her," Pete said from his perch on the fence.

"What should I say?" Chelsea's grip on the reins tightened, and Peony's gait stumbled.

"Whatever you want her to hear."

Chelsea didn't know what a horse should hear. "I moved here from Dallas," she started, her voice barely making it past her own ears. "I had a job there. Friends. A boyfriend."

Images of her downtown apartment paraded through her mind. The custom cabinets. The granite countertops. The stained glass in the front door. She thought of Hailey and Kim, her partners in crime. They'd introduced her to Danny, but she shelved the memories of him as she passed Pete.

"I can't cook," she said. "But I'm sure you smelled the evidence of that this evening." She turned back to see if Peony was listening. "I'm going to work on that, though. By the time Squire gets back, I'll be a professional chef."

Peony's head nodded with every step, and it seemed like she was agreeing with Chelsea. A tiny crack in her heart sealed shut with the presence of this animal, her gentle nature and willing spirit.

"Okay, put 'er in the center." Pete jumped down from the fence and gathered a large exercise ball from the barn. "Let's play pony ball."

Chelsea looped the reins around Peony's saddle horn, wondering if her leg would swing as easily over the horse's back as it once had.

Pete rolled the ball along the dirt, his fingers brushing the top every few steps. She wondered what his hand would feel like sweeping along the tender skin of her neck, her back.

Peony snuffled, as if reading Chelsea's mixed-up thoughts. She couldn't entertain the idea of having more than a friendship with Pete. The tan line on her ring finger testified of that. She'd already vowed not to make that mistake a third time.

From several feet away, Pete gave the ball a bigger push. "Ball, Peony."

The horse stepped forward, trapping the ball between her front legs. She moved and kneed the ball back to Pete.

Chelsea clapped her hands twice, enthralled by the horse. "I want to try."

"Come on over."

She collected the exercise ball, relishing the feel of dust under her fingertips. She'd spent too much time cooped up behind a desk, making marketing strategies and blowing smoke at high-profile clients.

Though she hadn't wanted to come home, she felt more complete right now, right here on the ranch, than she had in years.

She pushed the ball toward the horse. "Catch!" she called. Peony tossed her head and booted the ball back.

She jumped up, her arms rising in one of her old cheerleader moves. She rushed the horse without thinking.

She flung her arms around Peony's neck. "You are wonderful," she whispered into the mane.

It could've been her imagination, but she swore Peony lowered her head and hugged her.

* * *

PETE WATCHED the exchange between Chelsea and Peony, and he knew his horse was ready to work with anyone. If having a squealing woman with flailing limbs flying toward her hadn't scared the horse, nothing would.

Just as certainly, something inside Chelsea had been healed as well. He wasn't foolish enough to believe that all her injuries had magically disappeared, but he hadn't seen her dance, laugh, or smile until tonight.

I need this program to work, he thought, lifting his eyes to the stars. *Please, God, help me make this program work.*

Watching Chelsea rub Peony's neck, murmur secrets to her, and lead her back to the barn brought Pete more satisfaction than he'd thought he could feel. He could help people. People with mental disabilities. People with genetic disorders. Veterans like himself, with mental, emotional, and physical scars.

This was his life's purpose, and he knew it as well as he knew himself.

"We never got something to eat," he said as they left the barn.

"I'm okay," Chelsea said, the few feet between them like miles and miles.

"Why don't you eat?" He stopped at the edge of the yard, his cabin back behind the barn.

"I eat."

He didn't want to push her. He certainly understood the way someone could slip into a black place where neither eating nor sleeping nor living mattered. He saw the circles under her eyes, saw in her something that reminded him of himself during all the skin grafts. The glazed look, the helplessness that felt like cement in his boots.

"That might be why you're cold all the time," he said, unwilling to let the subject drop quite yet. He wasn't a psychologist, but he knew talking to someone aided the equine therapy.

"I'm not—"

"When I had my fourth or fifth skin graft, everything they gave me for the pain made me nauseous. Then those blasted nurses wanted me to get up and walk around. I think I convinced them to leave me alone when I fell."

He studied the skies, because Chelsea's gaze felt too powerful, too penetrating, too personal. "So if you faint, then I'll leave you alone."

"How many skin grafts did you have?" She maneuvered around to his right side and placed her fingers on his puckered skin.

He jerked away, the touch too much. Too new. No one

except nurses and doctors had touched his injury, ever.

"Sorry," she murmured.

Embers of embarrassment swirled through his stomach. Why was he rejecting her? Because she was Squire's older sister? Because he was sure that wasn't how Squire wanted him to take care of her?

Or because he was sensitive about his disfigurement?

He reached for her hand, guiding her down the graveled path to his cabin. "No, I'm sorry. It's just...well, no one's wanted to touch my lumpy skin. It scares them."

"Does it hurt?"

"Not anymore." His bootsteps scuffed against gravel, and his heart felt the same way grating against his ribs. "I had about fifteen grafts, I think. In June, they finally told me they couldn't do anything more."

Her fingers wandered up his arm to his shirtsleeve and back to his. He shivered, though he definitely ate enough and had no reason to have a chill.

"How far does it extend?"

With his free hand, he nudged aside his collar until he felt the rough skin it covered. "Up here." He dropped his hand. "And all the way across my torso, some on my hip."

Her head dropped to study the ground. "I don't have any physical injuries."

"Doesn't mean you're not wounded." The words slipped out before he could think. "I mean—"

"No, you're right." She wouldn't meet his eyes. "I'm fine, but I know some sicknesses aren't visible." She spoke with such tenderness, Pete believed she'd had first-hand experience with invisible injuries. He wondered which ones, and why they'd scarred her if she was fine.

He opened the door to his cabin and flicked on the light, releasing her hand as he did. "Well, I think I can whip up some pancakes you might actually eat." He busied himself in the small kitchen, well aware of her appraising gaze on his walls, his sofa, his small TV.

"You live here alone?"

"Squire and I shared until he moved." He measured the mix and the water, adding an egg.

"Why'd you add the egg?" she asked, settling at his kitchen table. "That's the same mix my mother has. The back doesn't say to add an egg."

"Something my momma taught me. Makes it taste more like homemade. Gives the pancakes more substance and fluff."

She watched him with those midnight eyes, sucking, threading, drawing him closer with every passing moment.

"So you wait until the griddle is hot, but not screaming." Once he started talking, he couldn't stop. "The batter should sizzle a bit, but not smoke." He ladled batter onto his hot griddle.

"Then, you see those bubbles? They cover the top, burst on the edges." He nudged a spatula under the first pancake. "When they do that, you know they're ready." He flipped the cake, and beamed at the golden brown color.

"On this side, they only need a minute." He flipped all the pancakes and then returned to the first one. "Done." He stuck the bottle of syrup in the microwave and stacked the pancakes on a plate. By the time he finished the demonstration, Pete didn't think he'd be able to swallow a single bite.

Chelsea did, though. She ate a whole pancake and reached for another. She didn't put syrup on this one, but slathered it with butter and reached for the saltshaker.

"What are you doing?" he asked.

"It's delicious. This toasted whole wheat pancake with salt? It's like a soft pretzel." She rolled the pancake into a tube and took a bite. "Mm, butter. Everything's better with butter."

He chuckled, comfortable and content to be here with Chelsea. As he walked her back to the homestead, the planets seemed aligned.

"You were great tonight," she said. "What are you going to do with your program?"

"I'm going to start working with Baywatch," Pete said. "Peony's ready. And I talked to Squire, and I'm going to purchase a piece of the ranch from your family so I can build my facilities."

She swung her head toward him. "Really?" The level of surprise in her voice didn't escape Pete.

"And I'm going to start nosing around town for volunteers, and I need to fill out grant applications and apply for the national veterans program...."

She stopped at the bottom of the stairs that led to the deck. "And here I've already caused a smoke storm. You're way ahead of me."

"Tomorrow, you can whip up the pancakes." He dug down to access his well of courage. "And if you're into it, we can drive into church together."

"Church?" Her nose wrinkled, those blinders going over her eyes.

"Doesn't start until eleven," he said. "I've been going since I got here." He ran his left hand up his right arm, still familiarizing himself to the puckered skin there. "It helps."

He didn't have to elaborate. She nodded, but she still radiated a *no, thank you* air.

"I'll think about it."

"You have my number." He stepped away from her intoxicating scent, her smooth hands, her broken spirit. Squire definitely didn't mean for Pete to start dating his sister. She just needed a friend—and someone to make sure she didn't cause permanent damage to the homestead.

Pete was happy to be both.

I'LL GO TO CHURCH, *but we're driving my car. It has air conditioning.*

Pete grinned at Chelsea's text, which came only a half hour before they needed to leave to make it to the service on time.

Breakfast is ready. Smokeless!

Pete grabbed his teal striped tie and pulled on his boots before heading over to the homestead. He'd slept fitfully the night before, not because he wasn't thoroughly exhausted and not because nightmares followed him into sleep.

But because of the woman standing at the stove, her back to the French doors, her dress hanging off her frame like a burlap sack.

"How much weight have you lost?" He entered the kitchen and slid onto a barstool. Blueberry syrup and a plate holding butter sat in front of him.

Her shoulders startled, but she didn't turn. "Just a little."

"That dress looks like it's two sizes too big."

"Just because it's not skin tight doesn't mean it's not the right size." She glanced over her shoulder, not to look at him, but so he could see her annoyance. He'd heard it already.

"Okay," he said. "None of my business."

She turned and placed a stack of five pancakes on the bar. They were all too blonde, barely a hint of brown at all. He took two anyway.

"I didn't let them bubble enough, did I?"

"They're a little light," he said. "The griddle might not be hot enough."

She nodded as she nibbled on a pancake without butter, syrup, or salt, only getting halfway around before she replaced the cake on her plate. "Tell me about your dad."

Pete's gaze flew to hers, to the raw emotion raging in the blue depths of her eyes. "He died during one of his deployments." Rapids cascaded through his torso. "My momma didn't want me to join the Army, but I did it anyway. Wanted to be the same kind of Marshall man he was." Pete pressed his eyes closed against the memories of their bickering, the constant argument that he'd die in the desert.

Pete had argued back that he could die on the way to the grocery store—something he'd wished he could take back a million times after he'd received word of his mom's car accident. The car accident which had happened as his momma drove his granddad to a doctor's appointment. Not the grocery store, but close enough in Pete's mind.

"I'm sure you're making him proud." Chelsea stepped away from the counter. "Be back in a minute."

She returned with a belt around her waist, which made the saggy dress accentuate her subtle curves. Her lips shone with pink gloss, and a silver bracelet dangled from her wrist. "Is it time to go?"

It definitely was. Pete stood and looped his tie around his neck. "Yes."

She slipped into heels in the mudroom, and he followed her to a luxury SUV. "Nice car," he commented after she'd slid into the driver's seat.

"Thanks." She focused on driving, her hands in the

proper position, her knuckles white.

"You haven't been to church for a while, have you?" he asked as she turned onto the main highway.

"Is it that obvious?"

"Yes." Pete chuckled. "You remind me so much of myself when I got here in June."

Broken. Uncertain. Lost.

Chelsea was definitely all three.

Pete had felt himself heal a little more with each passing day on the ranch. He had purpose now with Courage Reins, but he was still uncertain if he could be successful. His wages as a cowhand were fine for now, but insufficient for a family.

He hadn't given much thought to a family anyway. But with Chelsea's touch and acceptance of his injury, his future had been blown wide open. And that had also kept him awake last night.

Chelsea pulled into the church parking lot, but she didn't move. Didn't even turn off the ignition.

Pete reached for the door handle. "You comin'?"

"I don't think so," she said. "You go on ahead."

She stared straight forward, but she wasn't seeing what was right in front of her.

"I sit by your parents, usually," he said. "Come on in, if you want. I'm sure they'd love to see you."

He wasn't sure, because of the noise he made getting out of her car, but he thought he heard her say, "I don't want anyone to see me."

Chapter Five

Chelsea drove away from the church, her passenger seat empty just like her heart. She wasn't ready to face the townspeople, though part of her wanted to stride into that church on Pete Marshall's arm and make an entrance the widows of Three Rivers would be gossiping about for weeks.

She stopped at the city limits and pulled out her phone. She searched for veteran riding programs and found a wealth of information. From facilities in Utah to Illinois to Virginia, there were a multitude of services for a variety of disabilities, including things like vision impairment and weight control.

She saw the words "abuse and trauma" time and time again. Her anxiety skyrocketed and she tossed her phone into the console. She had not been abused. At least Danny had never raised his hand to her.

Sure, sometimes he said mean things. But he felt so much pain, so much anger, sometimes it came out. If it didn't, he would've died.

He died anyway, she thought, flipping the car into drive and making a U-turn. She entered the church, her steps light as she tried not to make any noise. The pastor lectured, and she slipped into the very back row so as not to disturb anyone. She thought she could sneak right back out before anyone saw her.

Pastor Scott spoke about the parable of the Prodigal Son who'd made mistakes and was still welcomed home by those who loved him. The passion in his words penetrated her heart. A strange feeling of love welled in her center, gathering and growing and gaining momentum until it spilled over in the form of tears.

Chelsea hated the feeling of weakness that came with crying. Hated it even more that she was leaking in public. She stood and hurried into the foyer, where she could still hear the pastor but didn't have witnesses.

A woman sat on the couch, a fussing baby on her lap. Chelsea averted her eyes without really seeing her.

"Chelsea?" The woman balanced the baby on her hip as she gained her feet. "It is you. It's me, Ruby."

"Ruby Atwood." Chelsea tried to smile, but it didn't fit on her face.

"It's Carter now." The woman smiled, and though they'd aged ten years, Chelsea saw the cheerleader Ruby had once been. Full of life, with a cute pixie cut to match her bubbling personality, Ruby had been a year younger than Chelsea.

"I married Tanner Carter," Ruby said like Chelsea should know who that was.

"Oh, congratulations."

She bumped the baby forward. "This is our little boy, Porter."

"He's adorable." Chelsea cooed at the baby, but her voice sounded tinny and false. The baby smiled anyway.

"I heard y'all were back in town," Ruby said. "How are you?"

"I'm fine. Living out on the homestead. My parents moved into town a couple of days ago."

"Oh, I know." Ruby might as well have waved her hand in a dismissive gesture. "They live just one street over from me. I took your momma a pie last night."

"Wow, thank you," Chelsea said. "I'm sure she appreciated that. Her kitchen isn't nearly as big as it used to be." She managed a closed-mouth smile that didn't feel seven shades of awkward.

"I have another one," Ruby said. "You want it? Y'all should stop by on your way back to the ranch." Her eyes seemed kind, her smile perfectly placed on her face.

Relief sang through Chelsea. Ruby didn't seem to know anything about Danny and his death. And why should she?

Because everything in Three Rivers runs through the rumor mill, she thought.

"Thank you, Ruby, but I certainly don't need a pie all to myself."

Ruby scanned Chelsea's body. "Sure you do, sugar. You look like you could put on some weight."

Chelsea crossed her arms across her bony chest. "Okay. Where do you live?"

The vibrations from the organ seeped through the wooden door, and Chelsea was suddenly anxious to wrap things up so she could escape to the car. But Ruby kept talking. And talking. And talking.

Chelsea edged her way toward the exit, but didn't manage to make it out the door before the members of the congregation started streaming from the chapel. Thankfully, that made it difficult for the conversation to continue.

Chelsea said goodbye to Ruby just as Pete made an appearance. His broad shoulders commanded the room, and the pleased expression on his face seemed just for her.

"Chelsea," he said, joining her. "You made it."

"For a few minutes."

Ruby gawked at Pete like she'd never seen a man before. "I'm Ruby Carter," she said, extending her hand as her husband stepped beside her. "This is my husband, Tanner."

"I know Tanner. He comes bowling with us sometimes. But it's nice to meet you, ma'am." Pete shook her hand and gave Tanner a man-nod.

"This is Pete Marshall," Tanner told his wife. "He works out on the ranch."

"Oh, no wonder you know Chelsea."

Chelsea didn't like the insinuation in the woman's voice, nor the way her eyebrows waggled like puppy dog tails.

"Yes, no wonder," she deadpanned, linking her arm through Pete's and pulling him through the door. She couldn't walk fast enough toward her car.

"Don't you want to say hello to your parents?" he asked.

Chelsea moaned as she turned around. "Yes, I do." But she didn't want to talk to anyone else. An impossibility, as every single person in town had heard she was back and they all seemed to have their Chelsea Ackerman radar set on high.

An hour later, she managed to start the car. She'd been sitting in it for twenty minutes as she visited with old Mr. Lyman through the window he'd tapped on just as she was about to make her escape.

Pete had been patient through all the visiting, smiling and introducing himself when he met someone from town he hadn't before.

She waited until her automatic window zipped into place. "Finally." She leaned back against the headrest and closed her eyes. "See why I didn't want to come in?"

"There'd have been a first time," Pete said. "Next time will be easier. And everyone seemed really nice."

Chelsea shot him a glare, though he was right. She put the car in gear and aimed it toward the ranch, stewing over how kind the townspeople had been. She hadn't expected that, though she wasn't sure why. Maybe she simply didn't feel like she belonged in Three Rivers, and assumed no one else would want her here either.

Either way, she "accidentally" forgot to stop by Ruby's for that pie.

* * *

"So, your mom used to make lunch after church," Pete said as she pulled into the garage. "Or we'd go to the picnic."

"Do you like strawberry yogurt? I have tons of that." She turned toward him in her seat, her dress riding up on her thigh. She tugged down the fabric and glanced at Pete, who had his attention focused out the windshield. The way he sat ramrod straight suggested he'd seen more of her leg than was appropriate. The slow flush crawling from under his collar did too.

"I'll grill something." He clawed at the door handle and scrambled from the car, striding away without looking back.

She sat in the air conditioning though her internal temperature had to be hovering only a degree above freezing. Had she imagined the connection between them? Did he not feel the same spark she did?

"Why does it matter?" she asked herself as she stepped into the blessed heat. "You're not looking for another relationship. Ever."

She marched through the house, out the French doors to the deck, and on down the steps to the yard. The horse barn housed the familiar and comforting smell of hay and horses. Peony's stall was empty, but the horse came trudging around the corner only seconds after Chelsea arrived, as if Peony sensed that Chelsea had come to see her.

Another horse came with the first, his coat a mousy brown mixed with white. "Baywatch." She patted him, wishing she had some sugar cubes for the horses. The tension and frustration whipping inside her stopped churning.

"I'm enough for you guys, aren't I?" Her whispered question went unanswered by the horses.

PETE GRILLED his filet mignon and green beans, a meal for one, before changing into a pair of basketball shorts and an old Army t-shirt.

He settled in front of his TV, the images blurring before his eyes as he thought about Chelsea. His food tasted like sawdust, and he didn't even notice. What was he doing? Going to church with her, talking to her about his injuries and afflictions, his family?

He couldn't get involved with such a damaged woman, even if she called to his nurturing side and made him feel like more of a man when he protected her.

After all, he was still trying to fuse the cracks inside his own soul. Playing the hero wasn't the same as actually being one. He knew that better than anyone. Not to mention his current housing conditions. He was sure Chelsea wouldn't want the top bunk in the cabin. No, Pete certainly had nothing to offer her financially or otherwise.

Friendship, he thought. That was all he could give right now.

A knock on his door alerted him to the fact that it had started to get dark. He got up and answered the door, expecting to see Chelsea standing on his porch.

She shifted from one booted foot to the other. "Hey."

"Evenin'."

She took a deep drag of air. "I want to go to the bank with you."

"Excuse me?"

"When you go to meet with the bank about a loan for the acreage you need for your facilities. I'd like to go with you."

He fell back a step. "Why?"

"Do you know what my degree is in?"

"No."

"Marketing," she said. "I used to be a senior executive at one of the biggest firms in Dallas."

"O-kay."

"I'm really good at filling out forms, and completing paperwork, and drawing attention to a specific project."

Pieces clicked into place. "You want to help me with Courage Reins?"

"Yes," she said, placing two fingers on his chest and nudging him further into his cabin so she could enter and close the door. "I think it could be amazing." She sat in the middle of the couch where he'd been, leaving him nowhere to go but right next to her. "I mean, I did some research before I came in to listen to the sermon, and there seem to be quite a few centers in Texas. But only one in Amarillo."

Pete stared at her while she spoke, his brain reeling with the meaning of her words. She'd done research? On equine therapy programs? During church?

"I took the liberty of calling them this afternoon, and they're swamped. You'd definitely have a lot of business once we get the program started."

He sank onto the couch next to her, his deformed skin forgotten as he took her hand in his. "I can start small now, while we wait for funding and start construction."

"Precisely." She squeezed his hand and grinned from ear to ear.

He sat back, unable to process and hold himself upright. She wanted to help him. He needed all the help he could get. "Should we go to the bank tomorrow morning? I think I can sneak away from the ranch for a few hours. I'll need to call—"

"I already spoke to Tom. He said it's fine."

"You already spoke to Tom. You called the equine therapy program in Amarillo." Pete's emotions tangled, and he pulled his hand away, the contact suddenly too intimate. Especially because she kept stroking her thumb over a wrinkled fold of skin on the back of his hand.

Every sound from the TV sounded like a shout. Pete picked up the remote and switched it off. "Listen—"

"Do you know why I moved back?" She stared at the now-black TV screen.

"No." He matched his quiet tone to hers, though he felt anything but subdued on the inside. His stomach raged, his heart rippled, his lungs reserved their air.

"I moved back to take care of the homestead so my parents could move to town and Squire could go to school." She folded her hands in her lap and looked at them. "At least that's the story going through the rumor mill in town."

"What's the real reason?"

"Someone very close to me passed away." Her fingers intertwined and released, braided themselves together and pulled apart. "A few months ago."

"I'm so sorry," he said, though he'd guessed as much from her questions and reactions.

"I thought I could fix him, and I couldn't." She gave a

light laugh at herself. "Stupid, right? No one can fix someone else. They make their own choices. Still." She shook her head as if she couldn't believe she was the way she was. "I like fixing things."

His spine stiffened as internal alarms began blaring. "I'm surprised you went into marketing. You should've been a nurse." That would've become the number one reason he would've stayed away from her. Pete was grateful for all the doctors and nurses had done for him, but he never wanted to see another one.

"I should be," she agreed. "I think I'd like it."

She had the eyes for it, full of compassion and easily masked.

"So I've realized I can't fix people," Chelsea said. "But I couldn't stay in Dallas. I tried for a while, but I was ready to go anywhere. When I called my mom, she said I should come home. I didn't have a plan, so I seized that one."

"You aren't happy to be here." He thought of her tears on the basement patio, so raw and so real.

She smiled again, but it wasn't happy. "No, I'm still working on that part."

"I felt like I was coming home when I got here," he said. "I want other people to feel that way, to feel the healing that comes from working with a horse."

"I want to help you do that." She reached for his hand, and though he resisted her, she muscled her fingers between his, her spark and internal strength shining through in her refusal to let him keep his distance. "Will you let me help you?"

She was asking more than that, but the questions remained a mystery to Pete. He felt them reverberate through his chest and lodge in his mind, where hopefully he could make sense of them later.

"Yes," he said. "I'd love your help."

Chapter Six

Chelsea proudly slid the bacon she'd managed to fry out of the pan and onto a plate. The smell had been teasing her for five minutes, but she suddenly found she couldn't put a single slice in her mouth.

She'd propped the French doors open, so she heard the footsteps coming up the stairs to the deck. She snatched a piece of bacon from the plate and ripped it in half. The other half went in the garbage with the remaining slices, and she'd just managed to take the tiniest of bites when Pete appeared.

"You cooked," he said, sweeping the kitchen like it had trap wires. "You didn't text me."

She put down her bacon like she'd just finished a huge meal. "I thought that was a joke."

"A grease fire is no joke." His eyes sparkled with a

tease as he moved toward the stove where the hot pan still sat and switched it to a cooler burner. "So, are you ready?"

He concentrated his gaze on her this time, giving her a once-over before meeting her eyes. "I feel underdressed."

She'd chosen a black and white striped maxi skirt and paired it with a sleeveless black blouse. He wore jeans and a polo, his cowboy boots and hat, and an adorable line of worry in the muscles around his mouth.

"You look fine," she said, almost choking on the last word. Her heartbeat betrayed her, but thankfully she managed to make light of the moment by saying, "It's the bank manager, not a mob boss."

"I'm asking for a lot of money." He removed his hat. "Maybe I shouldn't wear this."

"No, no." She reached for it and placed it back on his head. "It shows how serious you are. You're a horseman, and they wouldn't be caught dead without a hat."

A flash of a smile spread his lips, and Chelsea's pulse did cartwheels. She turned away from him to strap on her shoes. *What are you doing? Is this flirting?*

She'd held the man's hand last night, even when it was clear he didn't want her to. She studied the tan line on her ring finger and reminded herself of the goal: Secure the money for Courage Reins. Nothing more.

"I still get to help with Baywatch tonight, right?" she asked.

"Sure, yeah." Pete sounded distracted, distant. She caught him rubbing the stubble on his jaw, then scrubbing the back of his neck. She smiled to herself, and immediately told herself to *stop finding him so attractive.*

But his need, his drive, to help other veterans *was* attractive. The way he spoke of providing therapy for those with disabilities drew her toward him.

Now that she'd been away from the ugliness that had happened in Dallas, she realized she received joy from helping others, from supporting them, from sacrificing for them.

Too bad it took Danny's death to realize that, she thought. And she'd discovered she couldn't fix another person. Help, yes. Support, yes. Encourage, yes.

Fix, no.

But as Pete opened the mudroom door for her and allowed her to go through first, she didn't think he needed fixing.

He just needed money.

"Can I drive?" he asked as she rounded the front of the SUV. "It'll help settle my nerves."

"Sure." She tossed him the keys, but he didn't move past her. He opened her door and caught her wrist as she tried to slide into the car.

"Thank you." His voice sounded silky and sticky, like spider webs. He lifted her wrist to his lips, pressed a kiss there, and turned away.

Her pulse popped like fireworks, like gunfire, like cold bacon in hot grease. The ghost of his touch burned, and it wasn't until he started the car that she realized she'd frozen. With effort, she got in the car, her left hand cradling her right wrist so nothing else would touch it.

He started talking, but her thoughts meshed so she couldn't do more than nod and give one-word agreements. He silenced by the time they reached the highway, and Chelsea found her focus again.

"Why is this so important to you?" she asked.

"I said last night, I want to help other people feel the way I did when I got to Three Rivers."

She shifted in her seat and peered at him, this gentle giant of a man who had a heart the size of Texas. "There's more to it than that."

He tossed her a look through narrowed eyes. "Why do you say that?"

"Intuition."

"Oh, boy," he said. "My momma told me to watch out for a woman's intuition."

She laughed with him, the atmosphere in the car lightening with the sound of their combined voices.

"So is there more to it?" she asked.

"Maybe." Pete's grip on the wheel tightened. "I don't know."

"What's in this for you? Personally, I mean."

His muscles rippled from shoulder to knee, creating lines under his clothes that released as he exhaled.

"I need a way to make a living," he said. "Shoveling out horse stalls and feeding calves isn't gonna cut it."

"So you're looking ahead to a family."

He shrugged one shoulder. "If that's God's will for me. I just know I need to make my own way in the world." His eyes widened as he glanced at her. "Not that your parents aren't wonderful, and the job's great. It's just...." His voice faded into the wide sky and his jaw slackened.

"You want more."

"Maybe," he said followed by a chuckle. "You know, this isn't really helping me relax."

She crossed her legs, aware of how skinny they'd become. She needed to eat more than a greasy bite of bacon for breakfast. "Oh, excuse me, good sir. Would you like to play Twenty Questions?"

"Absolutely not."

Her laughter was a gut reaction, something she didn't consider before letting it fly from her mouth. It felt good to not have to worry over everything she said, everything she did, how her voice sounded, or how Danny would take it.

The laughter died midflight at the immediacy of Danny in her mind, like he was still alive.

He's dead, she reminded herself. She didn't have to censor herself anymore. She wasn't his emotional hostage. She wasn't a slave to his mood, or his scrutiny, or his constant need for reassurance.

"You okay?" Pete asked.

"Fine," she choked out, willing the panic back into the well she reserved for it. She would not ruin Pete's morning with an anxiety attack.

* * *

Pete watched the real Chelsea Ackerman fade behind a plastic face of perfect control. He suspected she was a wreck inside, though he wasn't sure what had caused it at this particular moment. The memory of her laughter—happy and carefree, and cut off mid-*ha*—floated around the car.

He wished he had more to give her, but his own anxiety had reached the boiling point. The session with Peony and Baywatch that night would soothe them both. *Just get through this appointment*, he coached himself. *Work on Chelsea later.*

He turned into the bank parking lot and killed the engine. "Okay."

"We can't meet with him out here," Chelsea said.

"Right." Pete got out and collected the manila folder of documents he'd prepared. The distance to the entrance seemed like miles. He put one foot in front of the other and arrived in only a few seconds.

He spoke to a woman at a desk, and she showed him and Chelsea into an office. They probably waited minutes, but it felt like hours to Pete until a petite, sharply dressed woman entered.

"Hello." She shook his hand and then Chelsea's, a smile giving her a softer appearance. "I'm Rose Reyes. I understand you're interested in one of our business loans."

Pete placed his folder on the desk in front of him,

trying to adjust his pitch for a woman. "Yes, ma'am. I'm looking to acquire land at Three Rivers Ranch and open an equine therapeutic riding facility." He pulled out a piece of paper, still trying to gather his thoughts.

"We'd have programs for veterans. My partner—" He indicated Chelsea, unsure of the term he'd just used. He wished he'd discussed the pitch with her. "—Has looked up the requirements to apply to be a PATH International sponsored center. We'd also appeal to those with Autism and other disorders, anyone with a physical disability, people with anxiety and depression, weight control issues, and those who've suffered abuse and trauma."

He removed another piece of paper and placed it on top of the business plan. "I need fifteen acres, and Squire Ackerman, the current owner of Three Rivers, has agreed to sell me the land for this price. We'll be partnering to use the horse barn, the grazing pastures, and the ranch's veterinarian time and feed supplies. I need a small office building, a large horse arena, both indoor and out, another pasture, and space for a homestead."

He took a deep breath, his tongue coated with stickiness and his throat dry. "Construction costs are nearly the same price as the land. But this is a drawing I made for the spaces I'd need, so we'll need to talk about a construction loan too."

He withdrew one more piece of paper. "When my momma died a few years back, she didn't have much, but she left everything to me." Pete kept his voice even. "I have a bit of money from that, but it's not much." He slid the paper with the meager amount toward Ms. Reyes.

The bank manager took the pages and examined them, spending the most time on the drawings he'd finished that morning. His nerves hadn't allowed him to sleep, and he'd spent most of the night with a pencil in his hand, sketching. He glanced at Chelsea, who had her cell phone out.

"How does an equine program benefit a child with Autism?" Ms. Reyes' gaze could strike fear in a platoon leader, and Pete set his shoulders.

"Many nonverbal Autistic children have spoken their first words after working with horses." He pointed to a line on the paper. "As you can see, I'd hire a psychologist to be on-staff to assist with some of the therapy, especially for patients with diagnosed mental disorders. We encourage our patients to talk to the horses, who have an uncanny ability to communicate with people, which helps heal their minds. Riding, of course, strengthens the core muscles in the stomach and back, the pelvis, and more."

She stacked the few sheets of paper and put them in the folder. "This seems like a worthwhile investment."

"My partner will also be applying for government grants," Pete said. "We'll be filing for non-profit status, and utilizing volunteers from the community to keep costs low."

"We'll also be seeking out donations," Chelsea said, her first contribution to the conversation.

"Let me get you the paperwork, Mister Marshall." Ms.

Reyes stood and started digging through a large filing cabinet behind her. She extracted two legal-size sheaves of paper. "One for construction. One for a small business loan." She placed a third on top of those two. "One for a donation request. Depending on the size of the project, how many people in the community it will impact, and the other applications we receive, the bank can possibly make a donation."

Chelsea swept up the paperwork, a look of sheer wonder on her face. "Thank you."

"And Mister Marshall. Save your momma's money." Ms. Reyes smiled. "It should be your rainy day fund."

Pete stood and shook Ms. Reyes's hand. "I'll get these back to you as soon as I can." He left the bank feeling fifty pounds lighter than when he'd gone in. His legs turned to clouds when Chelsea slipped her hand into his.

"Nice work, Lieutenant." She wore a grin in her words. "That pitch was perfect, and I don't know if you know this, but Miss Reyes has a daughter with Autism."

Pete stalled on the sidewalk. "She does not."

"Yes, she does. I texted my mom while you were talking, and she filled me in."

He dropped Chelsea's hand. "Be right back." He practically sprinted back into the bank, hoping Ms. Reyes hadn't vacated her office yet.

She hadn't. "Miss Reyes?" he said, much less confident now that he was face-to-face with her.

"Yes?"

"Okay, uh, okay look. Chelsea just told me about your daughter. What's her name?"

"Mari."

"Mari," Pete repeated. "How old is she?"

"Eleven."

"I wonder...I mean, would you like to bring her out to the ranch to participate in the training of the horses?"

Concern rode in her eyes and she frowned.

"I mean, my horses are ready, but I'm still learning everything my facility needs. I'd love to allow Mari to come for free so I can see what treatments might work best for someone like her."

Ms. Reyes nodded. "Yes, I think she'd like that. We have a dog, and she adores him."

"When can you come?"

"Tomorrow night?" she offered.

A grin split Pete's face. "Tomorrow night it is." He pumped her hand again. "Thank you."

* * *

CHELSEA SHOWED up in the horse barn wearing the same skirt and blouse she'd worn to the bank. He'd babbled the whole way home about what they needed to do next, and she'd promised she'd get the application forms filled out.

Pete had gone to work fulfilling his duties on the ranch, which included resetting several posts and feeding an entire field of cattle.

"You look tired," he said as she lifted a hand to pat Peony. "Did you eat lunch or dinner?"

"I'm fine," she said, which he noted was not an answer to his question. "I got your forms filled out." She lifted the manila folder. "And I got the applications we need for a couple of federal grants, as well as membership in PATH International."

"Great," Pete said, still peering at her like he'd be able to tell how many calories she'd consumed or how many minutes she'd slept just by looking.

"Stop it." She moved away to place the folder on a shelf before turning back to him.

"Stop what?"

"Analyzing me. I said I was fine."

"If you say so." He didn't think she was. She hadn't snapped at him since the night she'd arrived on the ranch. "Should I bring out Baywatch?"

She shrugged like she didn't care, but Pete knew she was ready. He needed to watch her, gauge her reactions, monitor her moods, to see how she progressed through her therapy. He hurried away from her before she found him appraising her again. She wouldn't like it if she knew he was thinking of her like a patient—like someone who needed help from the horses, not the other way around.

He released Baywatch from his stall. "Go to Peony." The horse ambled down the aisle, turning into Peony's pen.

Pete heard the gentle coo from Chelsea, and when he

joined her back at the rail, she had Baywatch eating a sugar cube out of her palm.

"Where'd you get that?"

"My brother told me where the secret stash is."

Pete nudged Peony back. "I don't want them thinking they get treats for the work they do."

Chelsea's fingers closed around the cubes. "I'm sorry. I didn't know."

"You think you wanna ride tonight?"

"No," she said so quickly, Pete wondered what she was afraid of. He almost asked. After all, she seemed to be able to push him to reveal personal information.

"Then I'm not gonna saddle them. Let's just put on a bridle. I'll do Baywatch, and you can suit up Peony. Deal?"

"I have to get them ready?" She stumbled backward, her chickeny legs barely able to hold her weight.

He reached for her but drew back at the lightning shooting from her eyes. "Yes, they need to be comfortable with anyone nearby. Anyone putting on their saddles and bridles. You don't have to if you're not ready."

She folded her arms, and Pete knew he'd said something wrong. "What?"

"This isn't about me, Lieutenant. Remember?"

"Of course not." The false tone in his voice could've been heard by a deaf man. "But they're used to me touching them and leading them. I need you to do it. If you don't want to, there's no point to tonight's session."

There was a lot more to tonight's session, but Pete

couldn't tell Chelsea that. As he'd suspected, she was not keen on being a patient.

She regarded him for several moments past comfortable, those arms staying clenched across her midsection. "I'll do it."

"Great." He tried to act like he didn't care one way or the other and went to get the bridles. He opened the gate and led her inside. "So take the muzzle and slip the nose down in." He moved slowly, clucking softly to Baywatch as he put the apparatus over the horse's nose.

Chelsea mimicked him, minus the vocalizations. Peony closed her eyes as if in rapture to be wearing a bridle.

Pete watched and felt Chelsea's discomfort and tension ebb into nothing.

"Now make her take the bit." He offered the bit to Baywatch, who took it without complaining. Peony also complied, but Chelsea's chest puffed out in pride. Or maybe she'd just taken a deep breath of relief that she hadn't lost a finger while jamming the bit in the horse's mouth.

"Slip the crownpiece on," he instructed and demonstrated. "And buckle the throatlatch."

Chelsea copied him flawlessly, her movements becoming more sure and her expression softer with each task she completed.

"Check the fit." He adjusted the cheek piece on

Baywatch so it wasn't so close to his eye. "And take the reins."

He checked Chelsea's work. "Beautiful." He ducked around Baywatch when Chelsea's attention snapped to him.

"Today, you'll be taking both horses out." He handed her Baywatch's reins and watched the color drain from her face. "Same arena." He nodded toward the back of the stall. "I'll meet you out there."

She lifted her chin and adjusted the reins in her hand.

"Not too tight," he cautioned. "You want them to follow you because they want to, not because you're pulling them."

"See you out there," she said, her step toward the rear exit hesitant. Neither horse moved with her.

Pete left, needing Chelsea to do this work, needing his horses to trust her even when her tension was palpable. Even though every cell in his body screamed for him to step in and help the beautiful woman who was helping him.

This is *helping her*, he told himself as he hurried to the outside arena. He just couldn't let her know about his double motive.

Chapter Seven

As Chelsea led the horses toward the bright lights of the arena, her legs teetered, her ankles wobbled. She should've eaten dinner. A piece of toast would've been better than nothing. She'd had a bit of watermelon after she and Pete had returned from the bank, unable to stomach much more than that.

The application forms called to her, and she'd spent her energy on them, researching grants, and going over Pete's designs for Courage Reins. He hadn't mentioned building a homestead, but it made sense. He'd need somewhere to live besides a five-hundred-square-foot cowboy cabin.

Baywatch tossed his head, and Chelsea repositioned her grip on his reins. "Easy, now," she said. "We're in this together, remember? Let's show Pete you know how to act." She glanced over her shoulder. "So none of that head tossing." She reached back and pushed on his shoulder. "And stop crowding Peony. Ladies first."

She swore Baywatch grinned and his eyes closed halfway in acquiescence. He waited for Peony to go first and followed dutifully. They emerged into the arena, and the sense of accomplishment flooding Chelsea made her lightheaded. The black sky above the arena spun and stretched and spiraled before it settled again.

She tried to speak, but nothing passed her vocal cords. Peony, somehow sensing her distress, stepped right behind her, her head bracing Chelsea's back. Baywatch came to her left side, shielding her view of Pete, who had once again perched on the fence.

"Okay?" he called.

She took two deep breaths and then two more. "No," she whispered.

Peony whinnied, and Baywatch snorted, one front hoof pawing the ground.

Chelsea heard the distinctive rhythm of Pete's boots running toward her before the blackness that existed beyond the arena covered her vision completely.

* * *

"Swallow it." Pete's voice echoed in her head, loud and commanding and endless.

Swallow it, swallow it, swallow it.

She forced her throat muscles to swallow whatever he

wanted her to. No one would dare contradict him when he spoke in that military tone, even her.

The liquid he'd given her tasted bitter, and hot. Coffee, without cream or sugar.

Someone else spoke, but she couldn't make out the words. She reached for the surface of consciousness, wondering when the dirt in the arena had turned into down pillows. She finally opened her eyes to bright lights, but not those outside.

Inside lights. Inside her bedroom lights.

She sat up, but Pete braced his hand against her shoulder. "Slow," he said. "Steady."

"I'm not a horse," she growled.

"She's okay, Tom," Pete called toward the doorway. "She just woke up."

Tom Lovell, the general controller, appeared in the doorway, a cell phone pressed to his ear. "She just woke up. No...I'll have her call you in a little while." He hung up and leaned against the doorway, though his worry for her rode in every line on his face.

"Your mom," he said. "She said you've never fainted."

Chelsea heard the accusations. "I'm just tired," she said. "We had a busy day." She met Pete's gaze, silently pleading for him to back her up.

"What did you eat today, Chelsea?" he asked, real low so Tom couldn't hear.

"Nothing," she said, causing his eyes to storm. "I'm

sorry, I—" she tried when he exploded to a standing position and paced away from her.

By the time he turned around, he'd caged his emotions. "You can't work with my horses if you're two breaths away from passing out."

"You can't take them away from me." She clutched the comforter to her chest, unsure of when the horses had become so important to her.

"Yes, I can." He circled nearer, like a predator to its prey. "They're not ready for someone to go fainting on them. It's not fair—"

"They did pretty good, actually," Tom interrupted. "They both spoke to you, alerting you of a problem."

"Tom," Pete growled. "Not helping."

"I'm just sayin' that maybe Miss Chelsea is the perfect patient for them."

"She isn't—"

"I'm not a patient." Her voice could've called dogs. Her gaze volleyed between a glowering Pete and a disbelieving Tom.

Tom shrugged and left her alone with Pete. He sat on the edge of the bed, very near her, very much where she wanted him to be.

He tucked an errant piece of hair and stroked his thumb down her cheek. She couldn't help leaning into his touch.

"Chelsea," he said evenly. "If you pull something like this again, I *will* take those horses away from you." He stood and crossed the room, only turning back when he reached the doorway. "If you don't want them—or me—to treat you like a patient, stop acting like one."

He stalked out, his boots thunking against her mother's hardwood. Male voices met her ears as her blood boiled and bubbled and roiled and raged.

She flung the blankets aside and immediately regretted it. The chill of the air assaulted her skin, but she tested her weight on her feet, glad to find herself still dressed in her skirt and blouse.

She followed the men into the kitchen, where Pete stood at the stove stirring something in a pot. "...always cold."

Tom made a strangled sound at the sight of Chelsea, stuffing his hat lower over his eyes.

"Chelsea," Pete said. "Sit down and eat." He pointed to the bar, and she stomped over to it. He ladled up a thick stew, with chunks of carrots and potatoes and beef.

Chelsea almost fainted again at the sight of it, and couldn't fathom putting more than a couple of bites in her mouth. He placed the bowl in front of her, a mothering look on his face. Well, mothering mixed with military, with a healthy dash of *eat-this-or-I'll-spoon-feed-it-to-you.*

"Thank you." She picked up her spoon and fished out a wedge of potato. She ate it just as he set a plate of bread next to her.

"Tom and I are stayin' until you're done," Pete said. "And I'll be making breakfast in the morning."

"I don't need a babysitter," she said, forcing the potato down her throat. "And this is delicious. You made this?"

"I don't get by on nothin'," he said.

"First the pancakes, and now this." She took another bite once the first had settled in her stomach without making it shatter. "Who taught you how to cook?"

"My momma," he said, passing Tom a bowl and dishing up one for himself. "She said I needed to be able to make myself a square meal." He took a bite of stew that had a piece of each item. Chelsea marveled that he could eat so much, especially at once.

"My mother tried to teach me," Chelsea said. "But she quit after the third meal where all we could taste was salt."

Tom snorted into his bowl. "This is delicious, Pete."

"Thanks. My momma said no Marshall man should have to depend on a woman to eat well. I was makin' bread by age ten and grilling corn on the cob that same summer."

Chelsea tried a carrot this time, savoring the rich broth against her tongue. Pete really did know how to season food to perfection.

He broke his bread and dipped it into the broth. She copied him, the garlic and butter on the bread making a party in her mouth. Before she knew it, she'd eaten her entire bowl. She got up to do the dishes, strength spreading through her limbs, making her mind clearer.

"I'm sorry about earlier," she said, looking both men in the eye. "I should've eaten before going to the barn. Is it too late to try again?"

"Yes," Pete said. "It's almost eleven, sweetheart." He scooped the leftover stew into a couple of her mother's Tupperware containers and stored them in the fridge. "I'm not joking when I say I'll be back to make breakfast. And remember Mari is coming tomorrow night. I'll need your help."

His eyes had never streamed with so much emotion. So much emotion that Chelsea couldn't decipher it all.

"Of course," she said. "I'll eat a truckload for dinner."

"I know you will," he said. "Because we're eating at my place. The three of us. Tom's helping tomorrow night too."

The seriousness of Mari's visit hit Chelsea with his words. She identified at least one emotion dancing in his voice: Desperation. He really wanted this to work.

"Seven o'clock," Pete said, heading out the door with Tom. Chelsea followed him to the French doors, gripping the doorknob as he descended the stairs into the darkness. Again, their voices floated back to her, but she couldn't hear what they said.

Chelsea tried to dismiss her growing feelings for Pete, but she couldn't.

She couldn't eat by herself, but she stomached everything with Pete by her side. Yawning, she collected the folder of applications and information she'd printed and wandered back to her room.

She'd ensure Courage Reins was successful. It was the least she could do for him, this man who had no family, who had come to Three Rivers and found his home.

* * *

PETE WOKE BEFORE THE SUN, showered, and headed over to the homestead. The windows were gray, a good sign that Chelsea hadn't tried to get up ahead of him and fake how much she'd eaten for breakfast. He'd found a pile of uneaten bacon in the trashcan last night.

He didn't know why she was starving herself. He didn't exactly know who she'd lost, or how long she'd need to grieve. But he wasn't going to let her work with his horses if she didn't take care of herself.

And that started with food.

He sliced thick slabs of bread and soaked them in an egg mixture to make French toast. He'd gladly let the horses work with her, but she still steadfastly refused to acknowledge the fact that she needed help. He wanted to ask her about it, but an opportune time hadn't presented itself.

He had several slices of toast ready when she padded down the hall, still wearing her clothes from yesterday. "Mornin'," he said. "Syrup or salt on French toast?"

"Syrup," she said, parking herself at the bar while he served breakfast.

Tom showed up a few minutes later, right as Chelsea finished her second slice.

"Mornin'." He loaded up his plate and took the third seat at the bar. "Cows in pasture four this mornin'. Horses in pasture seven this afternoon."

Pete accepted his work assignment with a nod. Driving to the pellet pickup, filling up, and then getting to the pasture took time. He'd have to make three trips to feed all the horses in seven. He'd be lucky to be back in time to shower and finish dinner before six.

"Thanks for breakfast." Tom replaced his hat and headed out.

"I better be goin', too," Pete said. "Those cows don't feed themselves."

Chelsea stopped him by standing up and holding her hands out. "Wait a second. I want to thank you."

"You're welcome."

She hugged herself as if cold. "Can I ask you something?"

"If I get to ask something in return."

Her gaze swept past his, unable or unwilling to settle on him. "How long ago did you get those burns?"

He rubbed his scarred fingers together. "'Bout a year ago, now that it's October."

Her lips pressed together as she tried to keep her control. Pete's heart cracked and seeped blood, but he had to ask.

"Chelsea, who died in Dallas?"

This time her gaze flew to his, bored into his. "My fiancée, Danny."

"Fiancée?" Pete had expected an answer along the lines of boyfriend, but not one that came with diamonds.

"I hadn't told my family yet," she said, running her

fingertip around her ring finger. "We were coming home for Thanksgiving. I was going to tell everyone then."

"I'm sorry," he said, though he'd articulated as much previously.

She waved his condolences away. "It's fine." She hiccupped, losing the battle against her composure. "You know, I'm not even that upset about it. He was very difficult to live with. Not that we were living together." She gave a little laugh, but it quickly morphed into a sob. "The first thing I thought when I got the call from the hospital was *finally, I'm free.*"

Pete's radar went off. He took a step closer to her, slow and careful, like he would approach a terrified horse. "Chelsea, did he hurt you?"

She nodded, then fanned her hand in front of her face as if to dismiss that admission. "Not-not how you think. He was-was...." She indicated the ceiling, like it held the definition of who Danny was.

"If you didn't want to be with him, why were you engaged?" Pete asked in an attempt to make the things she'd said line up.

"Can we talk about this another time?" She wiped her tears and made herself as tall as she could. He still had six inches on her, but he felt small when she made herself so strong. Especially because he knew it was a mask, a façade, a part she played to make it through the day.

He knew, because he used to do the same thing. Some

days, he still did. He'd had a year to come to terms with his new life. She'd had a few months.

"Sure, yeah," he said. "I'm sorry if, I mean, you don't have to tell me." He drew her into his arms and gave her a squeeze. "Just know you can, if you want. Chances are, I'll understand."

She pressed her cheek to his chest, and Pete's heart went wild. He envisioned a time where he woke next to this beautiful creature, made her breakfast, and kissed her before heading out to train his horses. Every day. Forever.

Right now, he only had this moment. Peace settled over him for two breaths before reality came roaring back. He released her and stepped away. "I'll see you tonight."

"Tonight." She sounded strangled, and he hated walking away from her when she wasn't one hundred percent happy.

He certainly didn't have time to be making three meals a day for a woman who had nothing else to do.

"Focus, Pete," he warned himself as he headed to his ranch truck. Chelsea was a project he couldn't afford to take on. He already had enough on his plate without adding a woman sporting a broken heart and a wounded spirit. Even if she did have the most captivating eyes. Even if she made him feel more alive than he had in half a decade. Even if she did inspire him to make more of himself than he thought he could be.

* * *

Exhaustion seeped into Pete's very bones, burrowing deep and biting with sharp teeth. He downed another mouthful of the strongest coffee he knew how to make, cringing at the overly bitter taste.

He sat at the table while Chelsea cleaned up. When he'd said he'd help, she'd insisted he remain at the table, claiming he looked tired.

"Mari will be here soon," he said, forcing himself to stand. "We should head over to the barn. Someone should always be there to greet the patient when they arrive."

"Let's go, then," Tom said. "It's nearly seven."

They headed out into the twilight, Tom in the lead. "Tom's going to monitor the horses," Pete said. "From a distance. He'll just be there in case we need him. I've been thinking...." He cast Chelsea a quick glance to gauge her mood tonight.

"You were thinking. Sounds dangerous."

He brushed her hand with his, quickly pulling it back. "I'd like you to work with Baywatch while Mari works with Peony. I'd like to offer semi-private sessions like this, with two or three patients. See how things go."

"Okay," she said. "You think he'll let me?"

"You did fine—I mean, he did fine last night." Pete cursed himself for speaking as if she was the patient, but she didn't call him on it.

He released the horses from their back rooms, pleased when they both moved into the stall where Chelsea leaned against the rail, talking to them. He watched her for a moment, utterly lost to the sound of her voice and the light in her eyes.

The crunching of gravel tore him from his fantasies. He opened the gate and joined her on the other side just as Ms. Reyes parked and opened her door. She called hello and moved around the front of the car, where she opened the door for a girl with the same bronze skin and dark brown hair.

"This is Mari."

"Hello, Mari," Pete said.

She gazed past him into the barn, where Tom waited out of sight and Chelsea hovered near the horses.

"Tell me about your dog," Pete said.

She said nothing, her eyes focused on something only she could see.

"Her dog's name is Paprika," Ms. Reyes said.

"Great name." Pete gestured toward the barn. "You want to go meet my horse? Her name starts with a P too."

Ms. Reyes linked her hand with Mari's and tugged her toward the barn. The girl went, and Pete followed, his heart hammering into overdrive. He tried to quiet the deafening thoughts screaming that he had no idea what he was doing.

"This is Chelsea," he said when they reached the stall. "And that white horse is Peony. You're going to be working with her, okay?'

Mari gazed up at the horse, her dark eyes full of wonder.

"Bridle them, Tom," Pete said. "Have Chelsea do Baywatch." He turned back to Mari. "You can come right in here." He opened the gate and entered the stall, Chelsea behind him and Mari and her mom following.

"Remember the nose," he coached Chelsea. "The bit. Good.... Crownpiece. Throatlatch. Check the fit."

Tom had Peony bridled in seconds flat and he handed the reins to Pete, who dangled them in front of Mari. "You get to lead her out."

His mind raced at the narrowness of the aisle. He didn't want Tom to go first, lest Peony follow him instead of Mari.

He moved to the back of the stall and pointed. "Right down that way. All the way to the end. We'll be there waiting for you when you come out."

The little girl wouldn't look at him, but he'd read that many Autistic children never made eye contact.

"Go where Mister Marshall said," Ms. Reyes told Mari. "I'll see you out there."

Mari moved, and Peony went with her.

"Chelsea," Pete said. "Wait until she's all the way out. Remember, we don't walk behind horses."

"Yes, sir," she said, and he wanted to thread his fingers through her hair, inhale the smell of her skin, and thank her for being so brave, so helpful.

He walked with Ms. Reyes through the barn to the arena, a much shorter distance. "Does she ever talk?"

"Only a little," Ms. Reyes said. "She loves her dog, and

her dad. She loves hamburgers and French fries. She'll sometimes talk about those things."

"Does she see her dad a lot?"

Ms. Reyes cut him a glance. "Is it that obvious that we're divorced?"

Pete ducked his head. "I didn't see a wedding ring yesterday or today. I didn't mean—"

She put her hand on his arm. "It's okay, Mister Marshall. Mari's father lives in Amarillo. She sees him every other weekend."

"Great," Pete said, emerging into the lit arena. Tom took a position off to the side while Pete climbed the fence. Steady, even steps sounded several seconds later, and Mari appeared with Peony right behind her. The horse practically nudged the little girl with every step.

"Walk her around the circle," Pete said. "And tell her about your favorite food."

Mari didn't speak to the horse, but she moved around the circle.

"Let's play a game with her," he said after she'd gone around twice. "I'll roll her this ball, then you do it."

Chelsea arrived with Baywatch, who had only used the ball a couple of times. Pete positioned the horses several yards apart and had Chelsea and Mari take turns sending the ball to whichever horse they wanted.

Mari sent hers to Peony every time.

Pete entered the ring and approached Mari. "Let's feed her. Hold your palm flat like this." He placed a sugar cube on the girl's outstretched hand. "Leave it still. Hold it about here." He demonstrated the low position. "Her lips might tickle."

He moved back to watch. Mari stepped right up to the horse, extending her hand and holding it precisely where she'd been told.

Peony sniffed the air and her lips wobbled as she suctioned up the sugar cube.

Mari yanked her hand back as soon as the treat disappeared, and laughed, laughed, laughed.

"Mom," she called. "Peony." She rubbed the horse's cheek, the smile never leaving her face.

Pete's throat narrowed. When he thought he had the emotion stuffed back where it belonged, he dared to look at Ms. Reyes. Tears streamed down her face as she clutched both hands to her throat.

"What?" he asked her, his voice catching on the soft spot in his heart.

"She never learns names that fast," her mother said. "And she always calls me Rose. She hasn't called me Mom for months."

Chapter Eight

Chelsea stepped from her air conditioned SUV to heat waves radiating from the pavement in the grocery store parking lot. She wished she owned wigs, could maybe disguise herself with more than designer shades and the wrong color of lipstick.

But she needed more than strawberry yogurt, so she gathered her courage as well as a shopping cart and hit the produce section. She managed to make it through the canned goods, meat, and dairy before someone stopped her.

"Morning, Miss Chelsea."

She turned to find Ruby Carter placing a bag of chips in her cart while her baby blew a raspberry and kicked his legs.

"Miss Ruby." Pleasure coated Chelsea's words, much to her surprise. She gave the baby boy a gentle pinch on his foot. "Hello, baby." A smile worked its way across her mouth and down into her soul.

She glanced at Ruby. "I forgot his name."

"Porter." Ruby swept her gaze across Chelsea's cart. "Looks like you're getting set for a while."

"It's a long way into town from the ranch."

Ruby nodded, her glossed lips curving up. "You have time for lunch?"

"Are you cooking?"

"Heavens, no," Ruby said with a giggle. "Porter and I try to go to lunch as often as we can." She tickled the baby, who laughed like a champ. "It's always more fun with someone who can actually talk."

Chelsea's stomach flipped, but she managed to muscle it back into place. Ruby didn't seem to care why Chelsea was back in town. Maybe she really did just want to converse with someone who did more than spit and coo.

"Where were you thinking of going?" she asked. "I haven't been back long enough to see what's still here and what's new."

Ruby pushed her cart toward the checkout stands. "There's Francisco's, the old pizza joint, but it's just as terrible as it was in high school."

A wave of nostalgia engulfed Chelsea. "Why did we think that place was so cool?"

"The dim lighting?" Ruby guessed, and both women laughed.

"Right," Chelsea said. "We couldn't see how greasy the food was and how decrepit the décor."

"I have no other excuse." Ruby began to unload her few groceries onto the belt.

"So not there," Chelsea said. "Is there somewhere new?"

"Newish," Ruby said. "You like Mexican? There's a fabulous salsarita that opened last year. The blue corn chips are to die for."

"Salsarita?"

"They make about a dozen different types of salsas." Ruby moved forward so Chelsea could load her groceries. "Tanner and I have tried them all. They're all amazing." She slid Chelsea a knowing look. "If I remember right, you like your salsa spicy.... Ricky grows his own jalapenos right here in town."

Chelsea's mouth watered, though she hadn't given much thought to actually eating at lunch. "The salsarita it is."

Ruby grinned like a cat who'd caught a canary. "You're going to love it, Miss Chelsea."

An hour later, Chelsea hugged—actually hugged!—Ruby Carter and promised she'd come into town every week for lunch.

She'd learned that Ruby couldn't do much cooking besides boxed macaroni and cheese and an occasional fried egg. It was better than Chelsea could do, and the two talked about finding someone who could give them cooking lessons.

Chelsea had sampled all twelve salsas and purchased three bottles to take home for Pete. Ruby had been right about the blue corn chips, but Ricky-the-owner also made the tastiest chile relleno Chelsea had ever eaten.

She placed her leftovers—half of the chile relleno—on the passenger seat and headed for the ranch. She sighed and relaxed, beyond relieved she'd been able to make a friend in Three Rivers.

* * *

THE NEXT MORNING, Chelsea woke to the sun warming her face, the smell of fresh coffee, and the wafting memory of a dream where she got to sit beside Pete every evening as they contemplated the stars.

Her cell vibrated, stopping just as she located it. Kim, one of her best friends from Dallas, had called.

Chelsea pulled her knees to her chest and leaned against her headboard. She'd promised her friends she'd give them a full report of how awful the ranch was. Only it wasn't so bad—at least not yet. She hadn't taken care of the lawn and living alone didn't generate a lot of cleaning.

She hadn't been bored because of all her work with Pete, and she'd made a real friend in Ruby Carter.

Her phone rang again, startling her as it buzzed in her

hand. "Hey, Kim." She made her voice as cheery as possible.

"Chels!" Kim's exuberant tone came through the line. "How are you? Are you surviving the overload of testosterone and cowboy hats?" Her friend giggled.

Chelsea closed her eyes and pictured Kim's blonde hair and baby blues. "I'm surviving."

"Sounds like just barely. How 'bout you come for the weekend?"

A healthy pause indicated that Kim was waiting for Chelsea's initial reaction. Her stomach tightened, and she knew she wouldn't eat for the duration of her time in Dallas.

"Sure," she said. "It'll give me something to do, at least."

Kim squealed. "We'll have the ultimate girl's weekend. Minus Hailey...she got engaged on Sunday."

Chelsea shot up like someone had inserted a rod into her back. "She what? Her and that guy from accounting?"

"Rob, yes," Kim said. "We're trying to be happy about it. She's over the moon, and doesn't want our opinion."

Chelsea heard the sarcasm, mixed with sadness, in Kim's words. "I'll be there. Maybe together we can talk some sense into her."

"I doubt it," Kim said. "I tried, and she shut me down pretty fast."

Chelsea got out of bed and began thumbing through

her closet for weekend wear in the city. "I'll be there Friday afternoon."

She hung up with Kim, her heart already heavy and she hadn't even left yet.

She left the packing for another time and strode toward the kitchen. She hadn't felt this good in months, and she knew it had everything to do with leaving Dallas, living without Danny, and meeting the handsome man in her kitchen buttering bagels before he placed them on the grill pan.

"Grilled bagels?" she asked, pouring herself a glass of orange juice.

"Bagel sandwiches," he corrected, indicating the sausage patties and fried eggs in the skillet.

"So that's what a fried egg should look like." She grinned up at him. "How do you do that?"

"It's all about temperature control." He nudged an egg closer to the center of the pan. "I'm willing to bet your pan was too hot."

"You'd win that bet." Her face felt like it could fry an egg, and she stepped away from the intoxicating scent of his aftershave. "So my friend Kim called and invited me to come to Dallas for the weekend."

"Oh?" He stacked the bagel halves and lifted them from the grill. "You gonna go?"

"I think so, yes." She watched him for a reaction, but he didn't give one. He assembled the sandwiches—three of them—and set them on a tray with a bowl of grapes.

"Breakfast, sweetheart." He indicated her spot at the bar. "Sit and eat."

Mild annoyance clouded her growing attraction to him. "It's a miracle I survived before you came along," she mumbled.

"What? I didn't catch that."

"Thank you for breakfast." She gave him a sugary grin and selected the smallest sandwich. She bit into it, a moan of satisfaction escaping before she remembered she didn't want to like Pete's concoctions.

"That's what I thought." He sat next to her. "You did great the other night with Baywatch."

Chelsea had a hard time swallowing. She finally succeeded, but the toasted bagel scraped her throat. "Thanks," she managed to say.

"How are you feeling?"

"What do you mean?"

Pete stuffed his mouth with about half his sandwich. By the time he finished chewing and had swallowed, the silence in the kitchen was suffocating. Chelsea knew he wanted her to drop the subject, but she didn't want to. Couldn't.

"Pete." She replaced her bagel on her plate. "What do you mean?"

"You fainted, Chelsea," he said. "I'm just wondering how you're feeling."

"I'm fine."

He exploded to his feet, the sudden movement

sending adrenaline through her in waves. His reaction reminded her so much of Danny's outbursts, the way he'd anger over the littlest of things, the way she never really knew how he'd react until he acted.

"You're not fine," Pete insisted. "Someone whose fiancée dies isn't fine. Someone who won't eat unless forced is not fine. Someone who suffers from panic attacks is *not* fine." His chest heaved as he sucked air through his nostrils. "So please stop lying to me."

He bent down, his face inches from hers. "You forget who you're talking to. I got blown up, okay? I felt those flames as they burned me. I know trauma. I know pain. I *know* loss."

He stalked away, one hand scrubbing and scrubbing and scrubbing the skin on the back of his neck until it turned red and raw.

Chelsea's mind spun, her thoughts and feelings tangling together the way they had when she'd received the phone call. When she'd quit her job. When she'd made the six-hour drive here. Why couldn't she think properly? Why couldn't she say what she really felt?

Had Danny trained that out of her after only six months together? She'd hidden how she really felt about things, in case he disagreed, in case her opinion would upset him, in case he'd then spiral into not being able to go to work.

"So answer me straight," Pete said, his back still to her as he stood at the kitchen windows. "How do you feel?"

"Angry," she blurted. "You make me angry."

"At least it's not *fine*," he said.

"I'm afraid," she said next, and the floodgate on her vocal cords broke. "I don't know how to feel. Did you know I couldn't express how I felt? If I did and it was wrong, things got bad." Her chest stuttered with a sob, and the few bites of bagel she'd eaten surged up her throat.

She gagged and coughed, her eyes overflowing. Pete strode toward her, his eyes edged with concern, but still guarded. "Keep going."

"I don't like it here," she said. "Or at least I didn't expect to. I like the horses, and talking to you, and—and—I don't eat because it makes my stomach cramp, and Danny thought I was gaining weight, and every time I think of putting something in my mouth, I think of what he put in his."

She gasped and covered her gaping mouth with her hand. She couldn't think of that, of him, of the way he died.

"It's okay, sweetheart." Pete held up his hands in surrender.

"It's not okay!" she shouted. "Just like I'm not fine!"

"What's not okay?"

Her brain bent, and bulged, and cracked, and curved. "He died, and it's my fault. I wasn't enough for him. I couldn't fix him." Tears splashed her chin, stained her shoulders, colored her collarbone.

"I wasn't enough for him." She shook her head, liquid

leaking from everywhere. Her eyes were so hot; her skin felt like carved ice.

"I'm not enough."

Pete gathered her splintered parts and held them together, his arms strong and sure around her. "Okay," he said. "It's okay."

She raged into his circle of safety, clawing at his shirt as she emptied her pent up emotions. He hummed, his rich baritone almost as soothing as Peony's presence.

But she didn't deserve comfort. Danny's death *was* her fault.

She pushed away from Pete. "I have to go." She hurried out of the kitchen, despite his calls for her to come back. "I'm sorry," she said as she pulled out her suitcase. "I just have to go."

* * *

PETE TRIED to get Chelsea to stay. To just sit down, for just a few minutes. To tell him where she was going. She wouldn't. She simply kept saying, "I'll be fine. I just need to go."

He watched her back out of the driveway and kick up a funnel of dust as she stomped on the accelerator.

"Stupid," he chastised himself. He shouldn't have pushed her. Shouldn't have insisted she answer him. Shouldn't have engaged in any conversation beyond the weather.

But Chelsea Ackerman intrigued him, and he didn't want surface conversation with her. He wanted more. How much more he hadn't considered fully yet, not with everything else he had on the line.

"You better go after her."

Pete spun to find Tom standing on the front porch. "You really think so?"

"She's distressed," he said. "What if she drives off the road? Hits someone else?" He tossed a set of keys toward Pete, who caught them out of the air, already moving toward the ranch trucks.

He called Chelsea, without a response. He pushed away his first instinct of panic. Panic wouldn't help her. Panic never helped him.

He dialed the emergency dispatch and described Chelsea's car. He really didn't want her to leave Three Rivers as upset as she was. She might never come back. His heart squished into a too-tight space inside his chest.

She had to come back.

"Can someone call me when they find her?" he asked.

"I'll send out Boyd," the dispatcher said. "I can't guarantee he'll find her, but if he does, I'll let you know."

"Thanks, Connie," Pete said and hung up.

He pressed the truck to go as fast as it could, coming onto the limits of town quicker than he ever had. He hadn't seen the hint of another car—certainly not a luxury SUV—along the way.

Please, God, he prayed as he came to an intersection. *Lead me. Which way do I go to find Chelsea?*

His first instinct was to turn left, so he did. A few turns later, he found himself on the street where Frank and Heidi's new condo was located. He blinked to make sure his eyes hadn't betrayed him when they saw Chelsea's car in the parking lot.

He skidded to a stop behind her, blocking her so she couldn't leave, and he sprang from the truck. Heartbeat booming beneath his tongue, Pete sprinted up the stairs and practically knocked down the door with his fist.

"Is Chelsea here?" he asked when Frank answered.

Sniffling and sobbing combined with the gentle voice of Heidi answered his question.

Frank stepped out and pulled the door closed behind him. "What happened?"

"I'm sorry, sir," Pete said, whipping off his hat and mashing it in his fists. "I pushed her too hard, I—"

"We expected she'd break down eventually," Frank interrupted. "I think my wife thought she'd be gone by now."

"It's only been a week," Pete said, his eyebrows drawing into a V.

"She's never wanted the ranching life," Frank said. "And it was very difficult for her to leave her life in the city, Danny's death notwithstanding."

Pete shifted his feet. He didn't like talking about

Chelsea like this, didn't like gossip at all. He preferred to form his own opinions, based on his own experiences.

"She's a strong woman."

"Yes." Frank glanced at the door. "She is."

"She fainted on Monday night," Pete said. "I asked her how she was, and when she gave me her standard 'I'm fine,' I pushed her to be honest with me."

Frank heaved a sigh. "Well, someone had to. She won't answer Heidi's calls, and I certainly don't know how to deal with someone who's gone through what she has."

"I feel terrible."

"Come on in, son." Frank clapped his hand on Pete's shoulder and opened the door. A blast of apple pie scented air met Pete's nose as he moved into the condo, and a rush of longing to see his momma, hug her, tell her he loved her, sang through Pete's soul.

"Are you stalking me now?" Chelsea's ragged accusation knocked him from memories of home.

"Just a concerned citizen, ma'am." He moved closer, her midnight eyes just as beautiful shrouded in tears. "You left so fast, and you were so upset...I wanted to make sure you didn't drive into a ditch or something." He conveniently left out that following her was Tom's idea, that he hadn't even thought of going after her. Like Frank, he had no idea how to deal with Chelsea's internal bleeding.

The horses, whispered through his mind.

Yes, he knew how to help her. Too bad it was exactly the kind of help she didn't want.

"As you can see, I didn't meet a ditch on the way here."

"Good news," he said, his mind whirring with how he could make amends here and keep her participation in the therapeutic program. "I'm really sorry I said such stupid things."

"Oh, don't go apologizing." She bumped him with her shoulder. "It'll make me like you, and I'm determined to be angry with you."

"For how long?"

"At least the rest of the day." She sighed as she glanced over her shoulder toward the condo's kitchen. "This place is so small compared to the homestead. I need to think."

"I know the best place to do that," Pete said. "And you can be as angry with me as you want. Scream to the sky and no one will hear you."

"Oh yeah? Where's that?"

"On Peony's back, on the wide, open range."

Chapter Nine

Chelsea followed Pete back to the ranch, helped him locate the camping equipment in the shed, watched him saddle Peony. Through it all, she kept up the ruse that she'd be going out on the range by herself.

Never mind that she had no idea where the cabin in section twelve was located. Never mind that she hadn't ridden a horse in over a decade. Never mind that he didn't even trust her to drive to town by herself.

She held no grand illusions that she'd be going alone. She didn't even *want* to go alone. She didn't want to go to Dallas either. She didn't know what she wanted, and that was a huge part of her problems.

"So when will you come to the cabin?" she asked him as he gave the final pat to Peony's flank.

"I'm not coming to the cabin, sweetheart. I have work to do on the ranch." He didn't wear a watch, or he'd probably have checked it. With her meltdown and subsequent departure, he'd lost most of the morning.

"The applications are ready to turn into the bank," she said, unsure as to why everything that came to her mind as a conversation topic felt wrong.

"Great," he said. "I'll take them by tomorrow or Friday." His grafted fingers worked a latch on Peony's bridle. She followed their movement, thinking about what he'd said about being blown up.

"I wasn't even there when my fiancée died," she said.

Pete's motion stalled; his eyes lifted to hers slowly. "I don't know what you want me to say."

She didn't need him to say anything. She just needed him to know.

"She's ready." He stepped out of the stall, leading Peony with him. "She knows where the cabin is." He retrieved a radio from the shelf and tucked it in Chelsea's pack. "Take this. If you don't get to the cabin after two hours, let me know."

Chelsea shouldered her pack. "And you're not coming."

"You said you needed space to think."

"Not about us." Chelsea wished she could suck back the words. "I mean—"

"There's an us?" His voice stayed as even as his gaze. Why could he look straight at her without a waver when she couldn't make her chest stop vibrating?

She hooked her pinky around his. "Of course there's an us. You called me your partner, remember?"

He pulled his hand back. "That's a business relationship."

His words stung, but she tried not to let it show. "Okay." She stepped up to Peony like she could get on the horse by herself. "Does this thing have an instruction manual?"

That earned her a grin. Subtle, but present. "Put your left foot here." He indicated the stirrup. "Push, jump, swing your leg over."

"Will you demonstrate?" Insects rioted through her insides. What if she couldn't get off? What if she had to get off and then couldn't get back on?

With the ease of someone who'd ridden horses his entire life, Pete placed his boot in the stirrup, pushed, swung, and landed in the saddle. Peony's ears barely flickered.

He dismounted with similar grace, and held the reins toward her. She wasn't sure, but his eyes held a hint of challenge.

Accepted, she thought as she practically ripped the reins from his fingers. With her left foot in the proper position, she attempted to push and swing. To her own surprise, she landed in the right spot.

"See?" Pete patted her leg like she was the horse. "Easy. See you in a couple days." He started to walk away, and the insects cocooned into moths and butterflies and locusts.

"Pete," she called, an edge of panic evident to all living creatures in the horse barn.

"Chelsea." He stood to her right, a picture of steadiness and surety.

"I can't go out there alone."

"Peony is with you."

"I—What if I burn down the cabin?"

"We didn't pack anything for you to cook, or anything to cook with."

How obvious did she have to be? Were all cowboys this thick?

"I want you to come with me."

His eyes narrowed, and he studied her like she was a perplexing puzzle he couldn't solve. "No, you don't."

"Yes, I do." She felt too exposed sitting on the horse while he stood below. She didn't like gazing down on him, though it did give her a thrill of power. Power she hadn't experienced in her relationship with Danny, ever.

"I thought you wanted to think. I thought you needed space." Pete stalked closer, causing the horse to lower her head and snuffle. "I'm the one who riles you up. I'm the one who upsets you. You can't possibly want me to come."

"I do." The childlike quality of her voice angered her. She wasn't the same woman who had been with Danny. Or at least she didn't have to be. That person could die with him.

She straightened in the saddle, infused life into her weak spots. "I like talking to you."

"Last time we talked, you freaked out and drove off."

"Fine," she said. "But if I burn down the cabin and half the acreage on the ranch, it'll be your fault." She clucked her tongue and pulled on Peony's reins. The horse moved down the aisle, leaving Pete behind.

Maybe some time alone would be beneficial. Maybe it would give her the chance to get her head in the right place, give her heart a chance to mend a little bit.

"The cabin in section twelve," she told Peony as they entered the sunlight. Chelsea adjusted her designer shades and set her sights on the wide sky. Only minutes later, the noises of the ranch faded into the breathing of the wind.

No wonder Pete felt whole out here. There was nothing between Chelsea and herself but the pure blue sky, the drifting clouds, and the rustling grass. Out here, she could be honest with herself. Out here, she could be who she really was. Out here, she had no one to hide from.

The thought was as freeing as it was formidable.

Only an hour later, a cabin came into view. Peony plodded along, stable and secure, all the way to the front door. Chelsea's core hadn't had such a strenuous workout in too many months, and she didn't care how she got off the horse, as long as it happened quickly.

She tried a reversal of how she got on, and managed to get to the ground without sustaining major damage.

The doorknob twisted easily, and inside, she found a square room with a pot-bellied stove for both heating and cooking. A long counter ran along the west wall, and a bare cot sat on the east. She wandered over to the counter, where a silver bucket waited.

For Peony, a note read. *Give her a handful a couple times a day.* The pellets inside hardly seemed like proper nutrition for a horse, but Chelsea didn't doubt Pete.

She lugged her backpack into the cabin and returned to unsaddle Peony. She took in her sleeping bag and the saddlebag with her food and clothes. After removing Peony's bridle, she set the horse to graze in the dry grass and returned to the cabin.

Five minutes later, she had the sleeping bag unrolled, the food unpacked and spaced on the counter, and the luggage stored underneath.

Without running water, Chelsea assumed there'd be an outhouse and a pump somewhere. She wandered around to the back of the cabin, where she found the facilities. But no fresh water.

An alarm started to whine in her head. Surely Pete wouldn't have sent her out here without drinking water.

She couldn't find a faucet. Determined not to panic, she returned to the cabin for her canteen. She drank and drank like that would make a well appear.

Still thirsty, she picked up the radio and pressed the button. "Pete?"

Several seconds passed before static came through the speaker. "Pete here."

"Is there drinking water at the cabin?"

"Yeah, around the back, near the trees, there's a stream."

Chelsea returned to the outhouse, and moved past it. In the distance—the great distance—a strand of trees broke up the skyline.

"It's like a mile away."

"Go once and fill up," he said, a chuckle sounding before he unclamped the button.

"Pete?"

"Yeah, sweetheart."

She smiled at the swagger in his voice, as she pictured him lounging with his boots up while he flirted with her. "It's less than an hour on a slow, plodding, girl-horse. You could leave when you get done with work, bring me dinner...." She released her thumb, unsure how to finish her sentence. Suddenly a kiss under this sky, with that man, plagued her.

"And then what?" he asked, his mood impossible to determine through the scratchy speaker.

"And then we can watch clouds and lie on our backs while the stars come out." The childhood pleasantries she'd enjoyed as a girl growing up on a ranch seemed like what she needed right now.

"I'll try," he said.

"Promise?"

"I promise I'll try. I have to go." The radio went dead, and Chelsea knew he wouldn't answer her if she called in again. Well, maybe if she said she'd started the prairie on fire.

"Might as well get some water," she muttered as she rounded the house to Peony. Then she remembered she'd unsaddled the horse.

* * *

PETE STARED at the silent radio, considering Chelsea's invitation. But he'd been to the single-room cabin in section twelve. He couldn't sleep there with her.

But he had a tent. And a horse. And a million reasons why he should stay away from the damaged Chelsea Ackerman.

Something pulled him toward her, his insane need to help her heal. He'd spent the few hours since she'd left trying to figure out what about her sang to him so strongly.

It wasn't her eyes, though they opened to her soul like pools of starlight.

It wasn't her magnetic personality, though she was easy to talk to, easy to be himself with, easy to enjoy.

It wasn't her sacrificing spirit, though he knew she didn't want to be at Three Rivers.

It was because she needed his help, and he couldn't stand seeing an animal in need, horse or woman. Though if he was being honest with himself, helping a beautiful woman was much more satisfying than assisting a horse.

With that thought, he knew he was sunk. He'd be saddling Baywatch as soon as his chores were done for the day, and he'd be in section twelve as fast as the horse would take him.

To stop himself from packing straightaway, he dialed his Army pal, who Pete hoped would be available to build his training facilities and homestead.

"Lieutenant Peter Marshall." Brett's voice came through the line with a vein of appreciation and amusement. "What are you up to?"

Pete chuckled and removed his cowboy hat to scrub his buzz cut. "Brett, how long you been back?"

"Long enough to miss your ugly mug." He laughed, and Pete realized he did miss his comrades in arms.

"You still doin' construction?"

"Yeah." His voice stretched like he'd been roofing all morning.

"You tied to Oklahoma City?"

"Right now, I am. Just finishing up a basement remodel for one of my mom's friends. What you got goin' on?"

"I put in for a construction loan for a homestead and horse training facilities." A buzz vibrated beneath Pete's skin, and a smile split his face. "I'm startin' an equine therapy program."

Brett whistled and scuffling came through the line.

"I'd love to come work on that with you. Where you located?"

"Just outside Amarillo."

Brett exhaled. "I'd love to get out of Oklahoma for a while. When does the job start?"

"Just waitin' on the loan."

"I've got nothin' lined up after this basement remodel, and I'll be done with that next week."

"I'll call you as soon as I know." Pete hung up, a spread of happiness flowing through him. He needed to get those applications over to the bank, pronto.

Unable to stall any longer, Pete headed over to the admin trailer, his assignment in the barns complete. He found Tom at the front desk, bent over a file of paperwork.

"The horses are happy," Pete said.

"Good." Tom leaned back and rolled out his shoulders. "And how's the princess at the palace? Is she happy too?"

Pete would've bristled if there had been any malice in Tom's voice. But the cowboy was as gentle as a kitten. More perceptive than most, which meant he knew a lot about everyone on the ranch, but kind.

"I sent her out to the cabin in twelve," Pete said. "She needs...time. Distance. More time." Even as he spoke, he knew he was lecturing himself. Chelsea needed a lot more time to heal, to grieve for her fiancée's death, to find her true self and embrace that person.

"So when are you headed out there?"

"Who says I'm headed out there?" He wasn't that transparent, was he?

"She's your project, ain't she?"

Barbs punctured Pete's lungs, and he sputtered. "No."

Was that how she felt when he slipped and referred to her as a patient? His project? No wonder her voice turned so shrill and her face so white.

"So what's next on the docket?" Pete's tone could've lifted clouds.

"Nothin'." Tom leaned back and grinned. "Everything's covered. Why don't you take the afternoon off?"

The afternoon off. Chelsea became his first thought, but a nap followed close behind. He could sneak in a siesta and still get out to the cabin in the early evening.

"Thanks," he said over his shoulder as he left the trailer. His cabin held the early afternoon heat, and a sweat broke out on his brow as he packed a duffle for his quick overnight stay. He'd have to be back before eight, ready for work, or Tom might think Chelsea had morphed into a different kind of project.

He decided to skip the siesta in favor of Chelsea's smooth skin. Just over an hour later, Baywatch nickered to Peony in front of the cabin.

"Hey, girl." He gifted Peony with a sugar cube from his pocket, which earned him a glare from Baywatch. "Settle down," he told the indignant horse and produced a second cube. He unsaddled Baywatch, brushed him down, and headed inside the cabin.

The empty cabin.

Chelsea had definitely been there, but she was nowhere to be found now. He meandered around the back of the cabin, and still she didn't appear.

"Chelsea?" he called, checking behind the outhouse and moving back to the front. His pulse kicked into a different gear when he got no response.

She'd radioed about water, and the horses needed to drink, especially Baywatch. He found Peony's bridle on the counter in the cabin and hooked her up. He took their reins and started toward the stream.

Halfway there, a stick figure appeared on the swell in front of him. He picked up his pace, making out Chelsea's dark hair after only a few minutes.

"Chelsea!" He waved one arm over his head.

She dropped whatever she was carrying and sank to the ground. Pete released the reins and ran toward her, his heart somersaulting from his throat to his guts and back.

"Hey," she said as she panted in the prairie grass.

He knelt in front of her, his hands automatically cupping her face and checking her temperature. "You okay?"

"It's so far to the water." She gestured behind her. "I can't carry that bucket another step."

"Bucket?" Pete retrieved the huge, silver bucket he'd asked Tom to fill with horse pellets and send out to the cabin.

He started to laugh, aware that Chelsea probably

wouldn't appreciate it. He dumped the water out and fell into the grass beside her.

"Oh, sweetheart, you take the horses to the water, not the water to the horses."

She pushed her bangs off her forehead and laid down, her eyes heavenward. "What about me? I drank all my water."

"You ride the horse and fill up your canteen."

Her fingers fumbled over his, finally aligning. She yanked, and he settled beside her. "Why didn't you say that when I asked about the water?"

"I don't know," he said. "Didn't think you'd lug a giant, metal bucket a half a mile to the stream."

"That, Mister, is a lot farther than a half a mile."

He squeezed her hand, tucking it closer against his side. "No, sweetheart, it really isn't."

"What'd you bring to eat?" she asked. "I'm starving."

"More of what I packed for you."

She groaned, rolled onto her side, and buried her face against her bicep.

Satisfied and feeling more complete than he had in years, Pete covered his face with his hat and enjoyed the lilting breeze flowing over his body—and the presence of the woman beside him.

"I'm going to fry out here," Chelsea said a few minutes later. "We don't all have fancy cowboy hats for protection."

He crunched himself into a sitting position. "Let's get these horses to water. Baywatch hasn't had anything."

"Peony either." Chelsea stood and eyed the bucket like it had bewitched her into carrying it filled with water.

"What did you do with the horse pellets?" Pete asked.

"Dumped them on the counter."

He must've missed them during his brief inspection. He collected the reins and led the horses to the stream, where they drank greedily. Pete scooped water into his own mouth, wetted his hands and ran them through his buzzed hair.

He sighed, his insides softening with the peace the range possessed. He'd been out here several times since arriving at the ranch, usually over the weekend when he didn't have duties. Once with Squire to avoid the fireworks. During that trip he'd had the idea for Courage Reins. During every trip out here he felt closer to God and closer to his center than anywhere else.

"What are you thinking?" Chelsea's question broke into his thoughts, welcome and unwelcome at the same time.

"Nothin' much," he said.

"You look happy." She smiled and dropped her eyes to the edge of the stream.

"I am happy." He moved to a fallen log and sat down.

"Even with all the scarring? All the pain you've been through?" She tucked her knees to her chest and gazed past the stream, into a reality that wasn't present.

"Yes," Pete said. "Those things are part of me now. They've changed me, warped me, formed me into the man I am today." He didn't want to repeat the tank attack, worked hard to keep himself from reliving it. But he wasn't sorry it had happened.

"That's what this life is about," he said, thinking of one of Pastor Scott's lessons. "God wants us to grow, and change, and become better. Every year. Every day."

"Mm." Chelsea scooted toward the water's edge, cupping her hand and letting the water drip through her fingers.

Pete leaned back and closed his eyes, letting the sun wash his skin and the wind cleanse his soul. He hadn't had this much free time in months. Normally, he liked staying busy. It kept his mind away from the more unpleasant things his brain settled on.

"You look too comfortable," Chelsea said.

Pete opened his eyes, but everything was too bright. So he didn't even see the palm full of water she flung his way. The cold hit him like a shock to the chest, stealing his breath. A jolt slammed through his blood at the same time she squealed and danced away from the stream.

He lunged toward the stream, gathered as much water as he could in his hands and flung it her way. He ended up getting more water on himself than on her, and his foot slipped on a rock, sending him to his knees.

His lapse gave Chelsea an opening, and she splashed and giggled as Pete's hearty laughter joined her lighter lilt.

"Oh, you're dead," he said, submerging himself fully in the water.

"Don't you dare," she warned, but the words held absolutely no threat.

He waded out of the stream, his arms folded around a pool of water. "Okay, truce."

"Truce," she said, taking a step toward him.

He half stumbled, half leapt toward her, wrapping his arms around her and wringing the water from his clothes into hers.

She wiggled as she shrieked, the indignant sound fading into a delightful squeal that sent a hot poker straight into Pete's stomach.

"You said truce."

"You started it," he said, his voice only betraying him slightly with its gargled quality. "I had to end it."

She stilled, but he didn't release her. His gaze flickered to her mouth, where a droplet of water slinked along her lip and dripped down to her chin.

He raised his eyes again, but she'd focused on his mouth. Pete's hopes lifted like helium balloons, but the rational part of his brain screamed at him to step back and give her the time and distance she so obviously needed.

He cleared his throat and fell back a giant step. His arms had never felt so empty, his personal bubble so cold. His momma used to tell him that the atmosphere only felt awkward if he felt that way, so he painted on a smile and climbed the bank.

He gathered the horse's reins and meandered back toward the cabin. Chelsea's sure steps sounded behind him, and her cool, drenched hand squirmed into his free one. "We better hurry back. Don't want to lose the light to invent those cloud pictures."

Pete squeezed her hand as his heart pinched inside his chest. This woman was carving a place inside his life that would be very, very empty if she chose to leave.

Chapter Ten

An unfamiliar sensation raced through Chelsea's veins. Something she'd felt before, but not for a long time. Probably not since she'd left the ranch as a hopeful college student.

The buzzing soothed her, brought comfort to frenzied places, water to desert ground. And it wasn't just the man walking beside her, reins in his hand. It wasn't the rush of flirting through a water fight.

This feeling ran deep, had always existed inside her. It spoke of love and acceptance. *She* was loved. *She* was acceptable.

She knew then that she had returned home. She really was like the Prodigal Son, returning home after wasting her inheritance. Instead of causing a pit to form in her stomach, as had happened at church, the hole inside her filled, and filled, and filled.

She wished Pete held the reins in his left hand so she could hold his right. She didn't know why she was so drawn to his injury, only that it grounded her.

He unbridled the horses, a task which required both hands, and she released him, hoping he'd take her hand this time. Her attraction to him had to be obvious, or else he held hands with every female who stepped onto the ranch.

Since Kelly had left, Chelsea didn't have much competition. Even the new accountant was male.

"So." He stretched out on the ground, his hands tucked behind his head as a pillow. "Tell me about the clouds."

She sat next to him, close but untouching. "There aren't many clouds today. This game might not work."

Pete's stomach rumbled. "Should we go eat instead?"

"Bring me something." The ground beneath her back was so unyielding, so dry, so cracked. It reminded her of her heart. Abandoned. Like a ghost town.

But just like the stream fed this part of the range, offered life, she felt her dry and barren heart softening. Beating quicker, stronger.

Pete stood and reached for her hand to help her up. "Come eat inside. It's too hot out here."

"The breeze feels nice."

"We can sit in the breeze when we watch the stars."

She took his hand—his right, puckered hand—and when she'd gained her feet, she released his. He let her go, and a flicker of disappointment fluttered through her. A sigh escaped before she could silence it.

He glanced at her, but she pretended to watch something else. "The range really is beautiful."

"Beautiful," he echoed, his voice like the whispering of the wind. He held the door open, his attention on her singular.

She stepped past him, her lips curling though she tried to keep them neutral. "So protein bars?"

"They're cookies," he said as the door closed behind him.

Chelsea unwrapped one, and it looked suspiciously like a cow pie. "These are not cookies."

"Beef jerky then." He pulled out a package and handed it to her.

"Our cows?"

"*Your* cows," he said.

She took a bite, tasting every flavor from the pepper to the smoke. "My cows are delicious."

He ate a protein cookie and tossed the wrapper in the trashcan. "Okay, well, I'm going to set up the tent before it gets dark. Don't want to miss the stars." His eyes twinkled, and she had a brief vision of watching them sink closed just before he kissed her.

She shook her head, her thoughts jumbling as her heart started tumbling. She couldn't believe she was considering kissing him. Thinking about it like she'd let him do it, let another man into the fleshy parts of her heart.

They'd barely started regrowing. She couldn't risk them for a kind cowboy just because he made her breakfast and taught her how to bridle a horse.

Even as she tried to dismiss him, the attraction to him grew. He'd done more than serve bagels. He'd shown her compassion. He'd accepted her. He'd cared for her, and he'd said hard things to her when he needed to.

He'd befriended her in a place where she was expecting to be isolated.

The door closed while Chelsea still sorted through the tangled ball of yarn inside her mind. "Wait," she called. "Tent?"

She opened the door to find Pete bent over a bulging bag and pulling out a log of fabric. "Why are you setting up a tent?"

"That cabin is one room, sweetheart. I like my privacy."

She swept his scars again, wondering how far around his body they wrapped. "It's hot out here."

"It'll cool down in a coupla hours. The sun's already on 'er way down." He snapped poles together, his capable hands working with precision. His tent came to life in under five minutes, and he placed his backpack inside.

"I'll feed the horses." He returned to the cabin, and Chelsea felt like they were performing a dance, one where they couldn't look at each other openly, couldn't say what was really on their minds, couldn't touch.

The disconnectedness gnawed at her, and she

migrated toward Peony. The horse lifted her muzzle from the nearly nonexistent grass and snuffed her lips along Chelsea's pocket.

"No sugar," she told the horse. She brushed her hands through Peony's mane. The hair was rough and comforting. "Why won't he hold my hand?" The horse's eyes drifted halfway closed, and Chelsea scrubbed her fingers along her neck to her shoulder.

"I mean, he must know I like him. I keep grabbing him like I need him to stand."

The horse harrumphed, and Chelsea gave a light laugh. "I know, right? Men. So clueless." She glanced toward the cabin and found Pete leaning in the doorway, his head nearly against the top of the frame as he watched her.

"Can you figure him out?" she asked Peony. "Maybe he'll tell Baywatch how he's feeling, and then you can tell me." She moved back in front of the horse. "Is that a deal? You'll eavesdrop for me?"

Peony's attention returned to the ground, especially when Pete started dropping pellets. While Chelsea didn't think they'd like them, Peony and Baywatch started scarfing their dinner like it was made of sugar.

"That'll keep 'em out of our hair," he said. Always one step ahead of her, he moved several paces away and spread a blanket on the ground. "Your starscape awaits, my lady."

She shot him a coy look as she approached and sat

down. "You always know exactly what to do," she said. "It's somewhat annoying."

He chuckled and removed his hat. "I'm good at details."

She patted the blanket on her left, and he obliged. As soon as he'd settled, she reached for his hand, tracing her fingers over the lines that were becoming more familiar. "That's why you'll do such an amazing job at Courage Reins."

"There are a lot of little details," he agreed. "But I'll need a lot of help."

"I volunteer."

He nudged her with his shoulder. "Can I ask you a question?"

Her muscles rippled and flexed. "Sure," she said casually, though she felt anything but.

"Why do you like to hold my injured hand?"

She dropped her attention to it, to the bright pink lines, the folds of white that wouldn't tan no matter how many hours he spent in the sun. Beneath what felt like wrinkled paper, she found strength in his tendons and bones.

"I don't know," she said. "I guess it reminds me that even the most damaged things can heal."

"You're not damaged," he said.

"Sure I am," she said. "But this hand—" She turned it over and traced her fingertip across his palm, where all lifelines had been erased. "This hand tells me that I can come out better. Maybe not perfect. But good. Strong. Alive."

As she spoke, an oasis sprang up in her core. Small, with barely a trickle of water, but present, and growing.

"You are good," he said. "And strong. I've seen the steel in you."

"Oh yeah?" She laughed. "Like when I was crying the first time we met? Or how about the panic attack that first night alone?"

Twilight fell, and Pete seemed absorbed in watching the sky gather darkness. Her frustration teemed inside at his silence. His silence that spoke of her weaknesses.

"Have you had another panic attack since that one?" he asked.

"Yes," she said. "This morning. You were there."

"That wasn't a panic attack. That was you, a rational person, running away from a difficult conversation."

"We can add that to the list of weak things I need to overcome."

"You're not a weak woman, Chelsea."

She appreciated him saying so, even if it wasn't true.

* * *

PETE'S EMOTIONS raged like brush fire, like bulls gone mad, like a river coming down from a high mountain. Chelsea's touch, the tender way she admired—*admired!*—his scars made him believe they weren't important to her.

At least not in a physical way, as something that made him less attractive.

He'd been on-edge since the water fight, since holding her so close and smelling the sweetness of her skin. He couldn't be contained in the same space with her, but sitting on the open range with so much air around them calmed his nerves.

She inched closer to him as dusk settled and the first star winked into existence. He pointed with his free hand. "Venus."

"My home planet," she said.

He smiled and ducked his head, coming within kissing distance of hers. She froze, but he looked up again, hoping for another interstellar distraction.

"Can I ask you a question now?" she asked.

"If you'd like."

"Why won't you hold my hand?"

"I am holding your hand." He squeezed to enunciate his point.

"Yes, but why won't you take my hand? I always have to take yours."

The truth rammed against the shields he had erected. The safety measures he'd built on his horse ride out to the cabin. The walls began to crack, crumble, crash as she leaned into him and laid her cheek on his bicep.

"Don't you want to hold my hand?"

"Yes," he said, his voice like a staticky radio station. "I want to hold your hand."

"Then why don't you?"

He spotted another star, and another, but they could not provide a suitable distraction. He suspected nothing would, so he drew a deep breath.

"Because, Chelsea, when we hold hands I want to kiss you." He touched his cheek to the top of her head. "And I don't think you're ready for that."

The sky deepened into night, a blanket of stars pinned against it. Pete's mind hurt from all the thoughts bruising their way from one side of his skull to the other.

"Pete?"

"Yeah, sweetheart?"

"Do you know why I hold your hand?"

Confusion puckered his brow. "Tell me again."

She straightened and turned toward him, clasping his hand with both of hers. "I hold your hand because it heals me. I hold your hand because I'm ready to move on. I hold your hand because I want you to kiss me."

His heart slammed into the roof of his mouth as he searched her eyes. Her deep eyes that reflected so much pain and beauty and strength.

His left hand curved behind her head to cradle her neck. He slanted his head and covered her mouth with his, his eyes falling closed just as their lips touched.

No shooting star would ever be as magical as the silkiness of her hair between his fingers. The world seemed to whir, whir, whir past him, but inside the bubble they shared, he took his time, moving and breathing in slow motion while everything else fell away.

PETE LAY ON HIS BACK, the ground beneath him cushioned by the sleeping mat he'd brought. He could no longer see the stars, but every time he closed his eyes, he replayed that kiss. The way her lips had trembled against his. The tears he'd found in her eyes after he'd pulled away.

"You make me feel loveable," she'd said.

He didn't know what that meant, and it scared him. He didn't love her. *Yet*, his mind insisted, just as it had for the past two hours as he'd mentally proclaimed his not-love for her.

He was definitely falling in that direction, and that made sleeping nearly impossible.

He finally drifted off, only to be assaulted by the bitter smell of burning metal. He thrashed, but his right leg wouldn't come free. The heat intensified, licking across his abdomen and tasting his chest.

He screamed, still unable to move his leg or get out, get out, *get out!*

Men called around him, the wind whipped the flames into monsters with sharp teeth. Monsters that ate slowly at a man's flesh, one layer at a time. Monsters that haunted a man for months, years, a lifetime.

In the distance, a horse whinnied, hoofbeats broke through the crackling pops of fire and the dying moans of men.

Confusion cascaded through Pete's mind, and he once again tried to free his leg. It moved, and he thrashed against whatever was binding him. It was so dark, and he couldn't see, couldn't see, couldn't see.

"Pete!" Cool hands stroked his forehead, tumbled over his neck.

"My leg," he moaned. "I can't get it free."

The sound of a zipper ripped through his nightmare, and he sat up, expecting the white hot, mind-numbing pain to slash through his body.

It didn't. The sound of his ragged breathing combined with the snorts of a horse, the pawing of hooves, and Chelsea's panting.

"Pete." His name came out as a whimper.

He scanned his surroundings, realizing slowly why it was so dark. He was in his tent, on the range. Not in a tank. Not in a fire. Not overseas.

"I'm okay," he said, but his tone wouldn't convince anyone. She scrambled around, finally locating a flashlight. The beam bounced around his tent, and he realized how close they were, how tight the tent was with a second person inside.

"I need to get out." He hadn't had a panic attack since arriving at the ranch, but everything pressed close, close, close.

She backed out of the tent, and he spilled from the opening, crashing into both Chelsea and Peony, who loitered a foot away.

He *breathed*, allowing the cool night air to cleanse his lungs of the smoke that had once clouded them. Peony pushed her nose against his arm, and he threaded his fingers through her mane, taking her comfort and infusing it into himself.

Chelsea wrapped her hands around his arm, like they were an English couple walking down the cobbled streets.

Her touch further calmed him, and the bands of tension wrapped around him like a mummy's costume released.

He exhaled, noting that dawn still sat hours away. "Sorry for waking you."

"I hadn't fallen asleep yet," she whispered, her breath washing over his bare arm.

"I haven't had a nightmare like that in a while."

Her fingers explored up his arm, crossing over his shoulder to where the scars barely touched his collarbone. She felt through his thin tank top over his torso, and all his muscles clenched. She pulled her hand back when she reached his waist and wrapped her arms around him.

The silence she allowed, the affection she so freely gave, brought him all the way back to center.

The night was shot, and when he nightmared in his cabin, he lifted weights, or visited the horses, or spent time researching and working on the concept of Courage Reins.

"You gonna stay out here another day?" he asked.

"No," she said. "There's nothing to do."

"You're supposed to enjoy that." He released Peony, who wandered away to rejoin Baywatch, and tentatively embraced Chelsea.

"I like the wide open space," she said. "With running water in the next room."

He chuckled as he lowered his head and tucked his face against her neck. Taking a deep breath of her powdery scent upped the attraction coursing through him. He suspected the contact with the horses was healing her, but that his affection would as well.

Hers certainly made him feel like someone could see beyond the scars to the man underneath. And that the man underneath still had worth. He wondered, though, if she'd be as accepting if she wasn't so entrenched in the hurt herself.

His barriers started to rebuild, but he didn't erect them quite as high. He didn't want to keep her at arm's length, even if she wasn't ready for a relationship yet. Deep down, he knew he wasn't either. Would he want to keep her up at night with his screaming? Never see her because he worked the ranch all day and trained horses and ran a therapeutic program at night? Rely on her for money until Courage Reins could support them?

No, no, and no way.

Though they stood in each other's arms, he felt worlds from her.

Chapter Eleven

Chelsea stood in the doorway of the cabin and watched as Pete mounted Baywatch. He brought the horse around as the sky turned from gray to gold.

"You sure you can get back okay?"

"If I can't, I have the radio. You'll be the first to know." She hugged herself against the morning temperatures. "Well, Peony will probably already know." She tried on a smile and it hitched into place easier than it ever had.

Pete grinned down at her, bent in half at the waist, and she stretched up to kiss him goodbye. "I'll take the loan applications in this morning. Maybe I can bring back lunch?"

"I never say no to a pretty lady who brings me lunch." He wheeled the horse around and trotted away.

A swell of happiness expanded her chest, making breathing easier and easier. Her mother had said coming home would be good for her, but Chelsea didn't think she'd been suggesting a romance with the most unavailable cowboy the ranch employed.

Pete's hesitance toward physical contact made sense to her, at least rationally. She held the same reservations he did, but her wounds weren't as easily seen. Still, she worried what people thought of her coming home, of her living at the ranch by herself, virtually the only woman within twenty miles.

She stewed over her trip into town as she cleaned up the cabin and repacked her overnight equipment. Pete hadn't had the chance to hover over her while she crammed one of those disgusting protein cookies into her mouth.

She'd get something in town. Eating had become easier here, far from the worries of her weight in Dallas, and miles emotionally from Danny.

She bridled Peony and got herself situated in the saddle—which Pete had put on before he'd left. The sun warmed her from the outside in, maybe the first time she'd had a normal body temperature since she'd put on Danny's diamond.

She'd known marrying him would be a mistake, but with him on his knee and that gem winking at her from the black box...she hadn't been able to say no. She'd even thought that once they were married, she'd be able to be more honest with him, that she'd be able to help him. And by "help him," she meant "fix him."

As Peony continued her steady journey back to the ranch, Chelsea let go of the self-loathing she harbored over how stupid she'd been. It wisped away into the atmosphere, where it couldn't infect her anymore. Though she'd been eating more than she had in a long time, she felt lighter than air.

She exchanged a glance with Pete as Peony entered the barn. Another cowboy met her and helped her down, his leather gloves rough against her hands.

"I'll brush her down," she told him as he took Peony's reins. "If you'll show me how."

"I'll get the saddle off for you. Put 'er in her stall."

"Thank you," she called after the cowboy.

She lowered her pack to the ground, her shoulders grateful for the lightened load. After entering Peony's stall, she watched the cowboy spiral the curry comb from Peony's shoulder and across her back. The horse snacked on hay and slurped water.

"Can I give her a treat?" she asked as the cowboy handed her a hard brush.

"Sure. This one likes oats. I'll get 'er some after I check her hooves." He indicated the brush. "You use that in short strokes across her body and back. She don't like it on her legs."

Chelsea looked at the brush, suddenly unsure.

"Start at the neck," the cowboy said, already checking Peony's hooves. "Sort of flicking strokes. Gets the dirt out and shines 'er up nice. Peony loves a good brushing after a walk." He gave her an encouraging smile and moved out of the stall.

He returned a few minutes later with a sack of oats. He poured a healthy amount into Peony's tray. "When you finish there, use the soft brush." He indicated a blue brush on the shelf. "She likes that all over. You can comb her mane too, if you want. Looks like it was windy last night."

Chelsea agreed that it was, and set to work dolling up Peony. By the time she finished, her arms ached and the need for a shower had become dire.

She leaned her forehead against Peony's. "Thanks for getting me there and back, girl." She took a deep breath, enjoying the earthiness of the barn and the heat from the horse's face. "Thanks for telling me about Pete last night."

She stepped out of the stall and headed through the barn without seeing Pete again. Two hours later, she'd delivered the applications and let her purse swing at her side as she meandered down the sidewalk.

The salon came into view, and birds rioted in her stomach. She didn't want to see anyone who would draw her into a conversation. Thankfully, Glenda stood with her back to the window, rolling someone's hair Chelsea couldn't see.

She bypassed the doctor's office and smiled at the kids running and shouting on the playground at the elementary school. By the time she arrived at Papa Henry's, the Italian place that had opened when she was a teen, Chelsea had taken enough of a trip down memory lane to last another decade.

She ordered a calzone before escaping to the park across the street. While she waited she watched the cars come and go at the grocery store. She snuggled into her hoodie as the park filled up with moms and small children touting lunches. School was in, so the crowd wasn't big and the children definitely small.

"Chelsea?"

She tore her attention from the toddler about to go down the slide and refocused it on the woman in front of her.

"It is you." The woman sat down, her heavily make-upped eyes scrutinizing Chelsea's subtle lip gloss and sweeping her clothes. Chelsea's fingers fisted inside her pockets, but she was glad she'd worn the baggy sweatshirt.

"Hi," she said, still drawing a blank on the woman's name. They'd probably known each other in high school, but she'd aged a decade in the past three months alone. "I'm sorry, I don't know—"

"It's Amy Harlow." She tossed her blonde hair over her shoulder and checked the playground. "Amy Garrison now. I married Phil a few years ago." She spoke like getting married was hard to do.

"Oh, I remember Phil." Chelsea's memories took her back to eleventh grade, when Phil Garrison got caught sneaking kids out of his father's grocery. Chelsea hadn't attended the party, because her mother could sniff out such things like a greyhound.

"What's he doing now?"

"He runs the grocer." Amy sighed like she'd faint any moment as she cut a glare across the street to Vince's. "He's busy as sin, but we're rolling in money, so." She trilled out a laugh that sent Chelsea's skin crawling.

"Avery, don't go up there." Amy stood and called to her daughter again. The little girl obeyed, and much to Chelsea's dismay, Amy plopped back onto the bench.

"So what are you up to?"

"I'm managing my family's ranch." Chelsea pressed her lips together, rationalizing the tiny fib.

"Heard y'all hired a new foreman." She picked at her nails, but Chelsea wasn't fooled by the nonchalant gesture.

"Yes," Chelsea said. "He's shaping up nicely." She hadn't met the man yet, but everything seemed to be going smoothly on the ranch, and it wasn't her job to take care of it if it wasn't.

Amy's smile would've scared a task force team, predatory as it curved her lips. "What did you do in Dallas?"

"Marketing." Chelsea wasn't getting paid the enormous salary to put up with princesses like Amy anymore, so she didn't need to employ her patience or use her placating voice.

"Rumor has it that y'all were engaged." She glanced toward Chelsea's lap, but the hoodie concealed her hands.

"Briefly," she said as her thumb stroked the place

where she'd worn her engagement ring. *Twice*, she added silently. No one knew about the first time, and Chelsea was going to keep it that way.

"What happened?" Amy leaned closer like the two non-friends would be sharing juicy gossip.

Chelsea's muscles bunched and released, screaming at her to a stand, run away. She stayed in her seat by sheer will.

"He passed away." The words scraped her throat and scratched her tongue, but she didn't feel like bawling. Her breathing remained normal. Only her heart had adopted a blistering pace, but Amy couldn't see that through the sweatshirt.

"Chelsea!" Ruby Carter appeared, casting a wall of shade on Chelsea. She collapsed on the bench next to her. "You here for lunch?" She eyed Amy with wariness, her tone a smidge too false.

"Just picking up." She adjusted her weight toward Ruby. "Weren't you tellin' me about a cooking class you went to?" She gave a little laugh. "I need to figure out how to do more than make pancakes." And if either woman knew she couldn't even do that.... Chelsea almost bolted right then.

Ruby's eyes widened, confusion evident. Chelsea blinked rapidly, hoping she'd get the hint.

"Oh, yes," Ruby said in a rush. "Your momma's been tellin' me about one for weeks now." She bounced her baby in her lap. "I haven't had time to go yet."

"Maybe I'll just ask my mom then." Chelsea inhaled and graced Amy with a smile. "I'm sorry, but I need to go." She stood and gestured for Ruby to come with her. "Come tell me more about how you made that pie without a cooking lesson. It was *delicious*."

Chelsea escaped with Ruby in tow, and when they were a safe distance from Amy's wolf-like ears, Chelsea sighed. "I'm so sorry, but I had to get out of there."

"I could tell." Ruby slid her a smile. "When I saw the two of you sitting alone, I knew I needed to intervene." She shuddered and switched her baby to her other hip. "Amy-the-Great cornered me at the picnic once. It was terrible, and Tanner refused to come over for fear he'd have to talk to her."

Chelsea glanced over her shoulder, but Amy had gone. "Well, thank you."

Ruby smiled and scuffed her feet in the dirt. "And, Chelsea, that pie was store-bought. You should be glad you didn't come pick it up."

The words took their sweet Texas time making sense in Chelsea's ears. She met Ruby's eye and guilty grin, and a laugh burst from her throat. Ruby giggled with her.

"I guess we both need cooking lessons. Oh!" She lifted a flashing, buzzing device. "My calzone is ready." She waved goodbye to Ruby before hurrying across the street.

While the people at church had been kind, Chelsea feared the rumors flying around town would elicit a similar scenario to the one with Amy she'd just endured.

Not everyone is like Amy Garrison, she told herself as she paid for her calzone. Heather James—Chelsea's lab partner from senior chemistry—rang her out, and she didn't seem interested in anything but Chelsea's credit card. Her smile was genuine, her tone polite. She hadn't asked embarrassing questions or boasted about her incredible wealth.

As Chelsea headed out of town, she categorized Amy as an outlier. Since Chelsea had come home, she'd made huge strides, emotionally and physically and spiritually. She wouldn't allow one woman to make her take precious steps backward.

PETE JOLTED out of a half sleep when a door slammed. He'd managed to mash his hat on his head and wipe the exhaustion from his eyes before Chelsea rounded the corner carrying a large paper bag.

"Three meat calzone," she announced. "Salad. Breadsticks." She began unpacking the food and placing it on the counter.

Pete noticed the overly large sweatshirt, the stiffness in her arms when she lifted out the bag of bread, the curve of her—

He jerked his attention away from her and out the French doors. The yard sat empty. The boys would all be eating in the trailer or out on the range, depending on their assignments. He'd finished a half hour ago, and the twenty minute nap he'd taken on the couch would be enough to get him through the rest of the day.

He stepped closer to her, his rational side warring with the part of him that wanted to abandon all reason and kiss her until he couldn't breathe. One touch of his hand to her swathed shoulder and his battle was lost. "Hey." He kissed her cheek, relishing the softness of her skin as she leaned into him and laughed.

"Hey, yourself."

His hand slipped to her waist as they stood side-by-side at the counter. He tucked her against his side, noting how well she fit, how easily she molded to him, how much he liked her there.

"The foreman asked me where I disappeared to yesterday," he said.

Chelsea startled next to him. "You didn't tell him?"

"I cleared being gone yesterday with Tom." Pete sighed. "But Garth wanted to know."

"Was he upset? Do I need to talk to him?"

"And tell him what?" Pete looked down at her, their eyes locking while he noticed the tiny space between them. "I took care of it. He said he didn't care what I did as long as I got my work done. I assured him I would."

She swallowed, her eyes drafting him, inviting him, daring him closer. His hand tightened against her body, and they turned toward each other as a single unit with a singular mind. She stretched up to meet his mouth as he dipped lower to taste hers.

He gripped her with a force he didn't know raged inside him. A passion that scared him more than anything else. He slowed the kiss, flexed his fingers away from her waist before gently kneading her closer.

The grin that broke their kiss was involuntary, and Pete felt its influence all the way to the soles of his feet.

"Let's eat." He stepped back and gathered a couple of plates from the cupboard.

She sliced the calzone with a serrated knife, beaming at him when she didn't sever a finger, and served him.

He ate with gusto, the packaged garbage he'd consumed for the past two meals nothing like real food. He noticed that Chelsea ate just as much as he did, but he swallowed his smile and kept the conversation on Courage Reins.

"Once the bank approves the construction, we can buy the smaller equipment we need," she said. "I priced the exercise balls and cones, the saddles and blankets so the program will have its own, that kind of stuff."

"How long does it take the bank to approve a loan?"

"Miss Reyes said the purchase loan will only take a few days. She has to call Squire, I guess, make sure the land is being sold for a reasonable value. The construction loan will take a little longer. Do you have a contractor in mind?"

"Yeah. I have an Army buddy who works for his dad's

construction firm out of Oklahoma City. I've already talked to him about maybe taking on my project. He said he was in."

"Maybe he can live on-site during the project. Is he married?" Her voice caught on the last word, but Pete forged on.

"No, he just returned home a few months ago. He wasn't injured in the attack and had to serve out the rest of his deployment."

"I have a big basement," Chelsea said. "Or he can bunk with you."

"I'll firm up details with him tonight." Pete stood and stretched, eyeing the couch, which made such a great napping spot. "I need to get back to work, sweetheart. Thanks for lunch." He brushed his lips near the corner of her eye and turned away before he couldn't force himself to leave.

PETE ARRIVED in the admin trailer just as Tom stood to start giving out afternoon assignments. He'd joined the swell of cowhands before Garth came out of his office. He scanned the crowd, saw Pete, and nodded.

Pete swallowed his discomfort. So he'd taken a single afternoon off—at Tom's suggestion—and gone out to the cabin. The ranch's cabin. With a ranch horse. But he'd had permission for all he'd done. Not Garth's permission though, and that was the foreman's issue.

Pete straightened his spine, determined to do things right by Garth. After all, he was the one here, running Three Rivers. If Pete wanted Courage Reins to be successful, he'd need Garth's blessing.

He took his assignment—moving hay from the storage barn to restock the horse barn—and stepped to Garth's office. He rapped twice against the doorframe. "Hey, Boss," he said.

"Pete. What can I do for you?"

"I just wanted to let you know that I've put in to buy fifteen acres of land from the Ackermans. Here on the ranch. I'm starting a therapeutic riding facility. Well." Pete removed his hat and scrubbed the back of his head. "That's the end goal. I've applied for a loan to buy the land, and a loan to fund the start-up of the facility."

Garth's eyebrows rose, his dark features turning harder with his surprise. "And the horses?"

"I included them in the bid for the land. Peony, Baywatch, Hank, and Juniper. The goal is for us to be partners, Courage Reins and Three Rivers. We'll share some facilities, like the horse barn and the outside arena, and when your working horses retire, I'll buy them and train them to work for my program."

Garth pulled a notebook closer and began scribbling on it. "Tell me more about this program."

Pete took a few steps into the office. "I have drawings

and plans, the ones I showed to the bank manager." He hooked his thumb over his shoulder. "Want me to go get them? They're just at the house. Chelsea kept them. She's helping me with federal grants and applying for acceptance into the national veteran's association."

"Veterans?"

"That's who the program will serve, sir. Disabled veterans, any vet who's been overseas. Anyone with any kind of trauma. I had a little girl out this week with Autism. She called her mom—" Pete chuckled at the shock on Garth's face. "Let me go get the folder. Then I'll start at the beginning."

Chapter Twelve

Chelsea hummed as she vacuumed, folded the blanket onto the couch, and wiped down the kitchen counters. Since she only lived in three rooms, keeping house had been easy. The afternoon had clouded, so she decided to forgo the yard work in favor of a good book.

She'd just cued up her device when her phone rang. Hailey.

Chelsea swiped open the call. "Hey, Hai." She giggled, like she used to with her friends.

"Chelsea, I heard a very dangerous rumor that you are coming to Dallas tomorrow night. I have something to show you." She singsonged the last several words.

"Oh, I know, I—" She cut herself off at the last moment. Kim must have told Hailey about Chelsea's upcoming visit but sworn she hadn't spilled about the engagement.

"I know I said I'd come, but I don't think I'm going to make it after all." Her thoughts wandered to Pete and what they could do together over the weekend. Surely he'd have some time off.

"Of course you can!" Hailey started listing all the things they'd do during Chelsea's visit, leaving Chelsea to fumble for excuses.

"I have to be here for church," she said.

"Church?" Hailey asked. "Since when do you go to church?"

"Since I don't have to work seven days a week, and since I have a very handsome man to escort me."

"A very handsome man?" Hailey said, her supersonic voice hushing. "Chelsea—are you, I mean...."

"Hailey." Chelsea took a big breath and prepared herself. "I'm not even close to the same person here that I was there."

"Okay, but that doesn't mean—"

"I wasn't me at all when I was with Danny. I'm not—I'm not sorry he died." Her emotion overflowed, but she managed to keep her voice even. "I'm happier without him, and while I wish he was still alive, I've released him—and the person I was when I was with him."

Hailey sighed, the kind that reeked of defeat. "You're not coming, then."

"I don't think so, little sis."

"I got engaged," Hailey said. "Surprise! The ring is gorgeous, but not as gorgeous as the man." She laughed, but the sound didn't carry the right level of happiness.

"Congratulations, Hailey," Chelsea said, though a vein of unease snaked through her. "Who is it?"

"Remember that guy that works in accounting at my firm? You met him a couple of times before.... His name's Rob."

"Right, Rob."

"You don't sound happy for me."

"I am," Chelsea said. "Really. Congratulations."

"You and Kim." Hailey laughed again, but this time it noised through the line like a bark.

"Maybe that should tell you something."

"What it tells me is I need new friends."

"Well, maybe." Chelsea had abandoned everything about her life in Dallas. While yesterday she thought she wanted to return to see her friends, she now didn't want to. She didn't want to go backward, even just for a visit.

"So if we're not going to be friends," Chelsea said. "Let me just say this: You can't say yes to a man just because he's gorgeous and the ring is gorgeous. Trust me on this one, Hailey. I've done it, and it ended badly."

"Rob is not Danny."

"I didn't say he was. But you won't be happy, just like I wasn't happy."

Sniffling came through the line. "Are you happy now, Chelsea?"

"Getting there," Chelsea said. "Are you, Hailey?"

"I need to go." Her friend hung up without answering the question, without saying goodbye. Chelsea leaned back into the couch, her heart constricting with concern for her friend.

* * *

Saturday morning welcomed Chelsea with the smell of sausage and the slow browning of toast. She ensured her pajamas covered all the proper parts and padded down the hall to the kitchen.

Pete stood at the stove, wearing basketball shorts and a tank top—his version of pajamas—and tonging breakfast meats.

"Mornin'," he said.

She yawned in return, stepping behind him and tracing the scars on his shoulder before wrapping her arms around his waist.

"Don't you sleep in on the weekends?" she asked, pleased that he didn't object to her touch, didn't stiffen in her arms.

"Nope. When the sun's up, so am I."

"Good to know. I'll start locking the door."

He chuckled, finished at the stove, and twisted in her arms. "It's time to eat."

"I don't think so, Lieutenant." She grinned as he gripped her body with his strong hands.

"Do I have to go all mother hen on you?" He pressed a kiss to her forehead.

Her pulse jumped, bounced against the top of her skull. "I don't need another mother." She leaned into the kiss he touched near her ear. "And I definitely don't think of you in that way."

She lifted her face to kiss him, stealing his strength and giving him whatever he wanted to take. She lost herself in his touch, the gentle way he explored without demanding. The first time he'd kissed her, she'd trembled with the trust twisting through her. The world had wobbled before righting itself, and the next time she looked at the sky, it shone bluer, brighter, better.

He made her life better.

Pete broke their connection, his face flushed and his eyes still closed, as if he was committing this kiss to his long-term memory.

"I adore you," she whispered, reaching up to touch his face.

His eyes jerked open, and Chelsea saw pure terror. He blinked, and his emeralds softened though the heat they carried didn't dull.

"I think you're somethin' special yourself, sweetheart."

If she hadn't been inches from him, she wouldn't have heard him. As it was, his words sounded like sandpaper against metal.

He moved out of her reach. "But we really do need to eat. I have a meeting with Garth this morning." He collected the sausage and reset the toast that had popped up during their exchange.

"Garth the foreman?" A pit opened in Chelsea's stomach. "What's going on?"

"Nothing serious." He plated for both of them and led her to the couch. "I'm keeping 'im up to date on everything to do with Courage Reins. It occurred to me that I'll need his help with my program. He'll have to deal with our construction, and we'll need to write up a contract about the shared resources and facilities. We're doing that this morning, and then I'll send it to Squire to sign."

Chelsea nibbled on her toast. "Can't I sign it?"

"Your dad passed the ranch to Squire," Pete said. "He's the official owner. He has to sign the official paperwork."

"I have some say," she said. "I got a percentage of the ranch in my inheritance."

"Only in salary," Pete said. "Not ownership."

Chelsea's throat turned to dust. "No, I have land too. Daddy said if I want to stay at the ranch once Squire and Kelly come back, I can build a second homestead."

Pete coughed, swallowing several swigs of coffee before he settled. "Really? Where?"

"I don't know." She crossed her legs and speared her sausage, unsure as to why her heart had suddenly started doing the tango. "I haven't thought much about what might happen in four years. It's too far away."

"Too far," he echoed.

"Though my front door will have blue glass in it," she said, brightening her tone. "I saw it once, on this charming cottage in Dallas. My apartment had stained glass, but I've wanted blue since I saw that cottage."

Pete nodded, and she appreciated his feigned enthusiasm for blue glass.

"So, after your meeting, maybe we could go to Amarillo. Do some shopping. Go to dinner...."

"I can't." He stood, groaning with the effort. "My Army pal is coming again tonight. You can help with the horses, if you want."

"Sure, that sounds fun." She just didn't know what to do with the twelve hours between now and then.

PETE KNOTTED HIS NECKTIE, whistling a tune from his childhood his granddad had taught him. Saturday couldn't have gone better. Early-morning breakfast with Chelsea. The heat of her touch against his cheek, the weight of her words—*I adore you*—brought him to stand still and savor.

He adored her too, but he was operating on unfamiliar ground now. He'd never felt as strongly about a woman as he felt about Chelsea, and he didn't know how to navigate such treacherous terrain.

She was still damaged—the way the horses worked more on her than she did on them proved that.

So he'd shelved her while he spoke with Garth. While

he cleaned his cabin and prepped for Reese's therapy session.

Knocking on his door brought him from his memories. "Comin'."

The door opened as he stepped into the hall. Chelsea's approval shone on her face. "You keep a tight ship, Lieutenant. I like it."

"I like *you*." He swept her off her feet, thrilled with her girlish laugh and how she braced her hands against his shoulders as she tipped her head back. He set her on her feet and brushed her bangs out of her face.

"I *really* like you." He kissed her, the cheerful tune from his childhood taking on a whole new meaning.

"Come on." She pressed her lips closed as she pulled away. "We'll be late for church."

He reached for her hand, securing it in his before they left his cabin. He wasn't sure if she was ready for much more than the kisses they'd shared, but then again, he didn't need her to be.

The service started with Chelsea a proper, public distance from him. She curled her fingers around his, and he felt her adoration. He felt like he could be loved. He felt like his massive scars didn't matter.

Peace flowed through him with the organ music, winding through his ribs and wisping down to his feet. He was in the right place, with the right person. If only she'd come to Three Rivers a year from now, fully healed. If only she'd come to Three Rivers a year from now, when he didn't have his hands full trying to start an equine program. If only she'd come to Three Rivers a year from now, when he had a sure way to provide for her.

As it was, he had a five-hundred square foot cabin and last Friday's paycheck. And a small "rainy day fund" that wouldn't last long if he chose to live on it. Chelsea deserved better. He wanted to *give* her better.

He leaned over. "I think Baywatch and Peony are ready," he whispered. "You want to help me with Hank tonight?"

She smiled, nodded, and leaned her head on his shoulder.

That night, she approached the big bay stallion with a level of calm energy Pete hadn't seen in her before.

"Slower," Pete said. "Let him come to you."

They'd started in the outdoor arena this time, and while Pete loitered on the fence, he'd put Chelsea inside with Hank.

The horse shuffled over, first sniffing her pockets for sugar cubes, the glutton. When he didn't detect any, he snuffled his displeasure at her. Pete saw her stiffen, but he also detected the shift in the atmosphere. He could feel her tension.

"Relax," he called.

Her shoulders went down, but she wouldn't turn her head. Her eyes tracked the horse as he rounded her. Pete had watched Hank interact with Squire, knew the horse had an uncanny ability to perceive where a physical injury lay.

But Chelsea was whole physically, and Pete cocked his head as Hank circled her again.

"I feel like he's stalking me," she said through lips that barely moved. "What's he doing?"

The horse punctured her bubble and almost knocked her down with a quick punch of his nose to her chest. She flung both arms out and grabbed his muzzle to keep herself upright.

Hank backed up a step, which helped her balance. She moved her hands higher to his cheeks and stared him right in the eye. "You're nothing but a big pushover," she said, laughing when the horse snuffled again. She glanced over to Pete, her dark ponytail swinging with the movement. "I think he's gonna do just fine."

"Let's play ball," Pete said.

She rolled the ball to Hank, who dropped his head and didn't know what to do with it. "Oh, come on," she chided him. "With your legs. Like this." She retrieved the ball and kicked it with her shin. It went bouncing over the dirt and she ran after it.

Hank followed her, a few long gallops at her side. Pete didn't know what to make of that, and he gripped the rails, hoping Chelsea could handle the animal coming at her.

"So you want to play?" She kicked the ball in Hank's direction, but he pawed the ground and ignored it.

"Run 'im," Pete called. "Take the reins and run 'im."

"This body doesn't run very well," she said, bending for Hank's reins. "But okay." She stepped closer to the horse. "Listen up, buddy," Pete heard her say. "I'm not a horse, so if this running is what you want to do, fine. But can we go slow?"

Pete swore Hank nodded, and Chelsea accepted that as his answer. She held the reins loosely—a skill Pete didn't have to remind her about anymore—and started running. Hank galloped beside her, their gaits mismatched and awkward.

"Too fast," she panted. "I'm a human, Hank!"

He settled into her rhythm, his black mane flowing behind him like Halloween streamers.

Pete jumped down from the fence and hurried into the barn to collect a saddle. Back outside, he whistled and horse and human stopped. Chelsea doubled over, her sides heaving.

"I'm going to die," she panted.

"It was three minutes," Pete said.

"You run at horse speed for three minutes."

"He wants to be ridden. And you're just the woman to ride him."

Chapter Thirteen

As if Chelsea's heart weren't palpitating enough. "No." She shook her head because she didn't have enough oxygen to form additional words. "No."

"Yes." Pete grinned at her as he tossed a blanket over Hank's back. "You rode Peony. You can ride."

"He's ten times taller than Peony."

"Ten times?" Pete scoffed. "You're a fine specimen, Hank." He scrubbed the horse's neck. "But you're not ten times taller than Peony."

"Pete, I am not riding him."

"Chelsea, I need you." Pete paused in his work, his shoulders drooping a fraction. "I really need you."

"Why me? Why can't you ride him?" Desperation coated every syllable.

"I've ridden him before. He's used to me."

She cocked her hip and didn't miss the twitching of his

lips at her sassy stance. "That's a lame excuse, Lieutenant."

Pete resumed saddling Hank. "He's responding to you in a way he's never responded to me. Please, Chels."

Her nickname rolled out of his throat, causing her heart to take a hop, skip, and jump to double its rate. "You're not playing fair."

"Nope." He grinned as he finished with Hank and held out a helmet for her. "Now come over here. I'll help you up."

"I'll help *you* up," she grumbled, but she placed her hand in his. She sucked in a tight breath as his hand settled on her hip. He was going to have to drive her to the hospital if he kept at it. She met his gaze, and she would've kissed him if they weren't out in the open.

"Thank you," he said, the words drifting between them with a quiet intensity. "Up you go."

She jumped and he lifted, and she landed in the saddle without an issue. Hank startled, and reared, and Pete yanked the reins. "Hey, there," he said.

Chelsea gripped the saddle, panic flowing freely now. Her breathing tripled, her pulse tripped, her chest tightened.

Hank tossed his head again, not getting very far with the grip Pete had.

"Steady," he said, and Chelsea seized on the calm energy in his voice as she buckled on the helmet. He slowly handed the reins to Chelsea. "He'll be fine, sweetheart. Give me sec to get out of the way. Then let 'im run."

"Let him run?" Her voice sounded like a cartoon character. "With me on him?"

Pete nodded and headed to his spot on the fence. By the time he regained his perch, Hank was prancing around the arena like he wore a crown and had a crowd of royal admirers.

Chelsea sat straight and tall, bouncing in the saddle with each stride. She leaned from the waist and gave Hank a pat on the side of his neck, crooning into his ear, "Good boy."

She kept her cool when Hank began to trot, and then to gallop. Chelsea hung on for dear life, a burst of adrenaline pouring through her, spilling from her in the form of a laugh.

She leaned into his neck, her hair flapping behind her, as Hank showed her what it was like to fly. She couldn't stop smiling, even though her ankle twisted when she slid off the horse's back.

Pete made her lead Hank back to his stall, remove the saddle, and brush him down. He really was ten times bigger than Peony, a fact her arms screamed with every brush stroke.

"You're a natural with him," Pete said from outside the stall. "Squire will be jealous when he gets back. Hank was one of his favorites."

"That's because he's just a big marshmallow." She giggled at Hank. "Aren't you, big fella?"

"He's really done a great job." Pete folded his arms and leaned into them.

Chelsea's brush strokes slowed as his words burrowed into her ears. "*He's* done a great job?" She turned toward Pete, and he straightened, his eyes wide and polished like sea glass.

"Training is hard work for a horse." The false quality in his voice made her eyes narrow.

The soft brush fell from her fingers as realization hit her. Pete held up his hands, as if he sensed the approaching storm and could hold it back with such a simple gesture.

"Chels—"

"You still think of me as the patient in these, these—" She waved her hands toward the arena. "These excursions. You're practicing with your horses. On me. Like I'm broken, or wounded, or *scarred.*"

"That is *not* what I'm doing." His jaw set itself into a square; a muscle near his eye jumped.

"Tell me, then. What am I to you?" A pain started in the middle of her chest, just below her breastbone, like someone had pieced her with a knife and was slowly making the hole bigger by twisting.

"I don't know how to answer that."

"You don't know how to answer that?" She chuckled,

wishing it was a light moment, a moment leading up to a kiss. "Not that simple, right?"

"Please don't do this. I don't think of you as a patient."

"You do!" Hank pranced away from her, and she stomped out of his stall, confronting Pete head-on. "You always have. You think I'm broken, and the horses are helping put me back together." Her eyes filled with water.

"Is that the worst thing on the planet? To want to help you?"

Her chin trembled, and she hated the weakness she couldn't conceal. "I don't want to be your patient." She swiped at her eyes.

He cupped her face in his hands, his touch gentle and firm at the same time. "I want to take care of you."

"You can't fix me."

"The horses help you. It's okay to admit that."

Why couldn't she admit it? They *had* helped her, sealed fissures in her soul and erased cracks in her heart. But Pete had played a big part in that process too. And rediscovering her faith had helped as well. She wasn't foolish enough to believe she was all the way better, but "I do not want to be your project."

"You're not."

She stepped clear of his touch. "Then what am I?"

He exhaled and removed his hat, his eyes trained on the dirt at his feet.

"Why can't you answer the question?"

He looked at her openly, and she could see all the way inside him. He was real, and strong, and beautiful.

"I'd call you my girlfriend, but we haven't really talked about our future plans," he said. "And girlfriend indicates a long-term relationship we're both enjoying, and both looking forward to continuing." He took a step toward her, but she fell back to maintain the distance between them.

Girlfriend sounded great, but Chelsea didn't like the label. The permanency it carried also brought fear, uncertainty. The band of skin on her left ring finger tingled, screaming about the pact she'd made with herself never to get engaged again. And *girlfriend* led to *fiancée.*

"So I don't know how to classify you," he said, each word coated with frustration. "I care about you. I want to help you, yes. If that makes me the bad guy, I guess I'll take it." He reached for her hand and twined his scarred fingers with her whole ones. "Please don't make me take it, though."

"I don't want to be the woman helping you with your equine project publicly, and kissing you privately."

"This is about more than that." His voice was so low, she barely heard him. The emotion his words carried slapped her full in the face, though. "You have to know this is about more than that."

"Define *this.*"

He lifted their joined hands, his right eyebrow cocked. "This. And me kissing you. It's not just a joyride. I'm not fifteen years old."

Oh, she knew precisely how old he was. He approached every situation with a level head, with a critical eye, with military precision. She should've been glad he was so predictable, so Army-like. But she wasn't a situation, and she didn't need his therapy.

Still, his emerald green eyes sucked at her, pleaded with her to understand. "Okay," she said. "And just so you know, I'm not fifteen either."

"I can see that, sweetheart."

* * *

PETE WORKED, and slept, and trained horses. He made sure Chelsea didn't try to make anything beyond a turkey sandwich, but he didn't have time to make her a hot breakfast every morning. He saw her every day, usually when she wandered out to the horse barn in the morning, or when he trained with Hank and Juniper in the evening.

She didn't volunteer to ride them or bridle them. She didn't even speak to them the way she used to. She was receptive to Pete's conversation, his kisses, his hand in hers when he walked her back to the homestead.

But by the weekend, the band of pressure around Pete's forehead was near the snapping point. He couldn't sleep past dawn on Saturday morning, and headed over to the homestead though he knew Chelsea wouldn't be up for hours.

She'd decorated the front porch, deck, kitchen, and

living room for Halloween, which reminded Pete of his momma and her love of holidays. A pang of homesickness pierced him, making his step falter.

His momma would've liked Chelsea, smiled at her spunk, advised Pete not to let a woman like her get away.

He paused outside the French doors, his thoughts running rampant. Was he letting Chelsea put too much distance between them because of his equine therapy program?

Standing there, pulse pounding, mouth dry, Pete knew she'd pulled back. And he'd let her. He'd let her sit on the fence, let her disappear inside the homestead, let her pour her own bowl of cereal.

I don't have any more to give her, he thought, tilting his face heavenward. *I'm already overwhelmed with my ranch duties and Courage Reins.* He couldn't add more hours to the day. Couldn't make his body need less sleep and less food. Couldn't force her to train with Hank—something that was mutually beneficial for both horse and woman.

He closed his eyes and said a quick prayer for strength, physical and mental, and entered the house. He could've lounged on his own couch, watched his own TV. But something about being in the same space as Chelsea brought balm to his nerves he couldn't get anywhere else.

By the time she emerged from her bedroom, he'd napped for an hour and whipped up a pan of baked French toast.

"Mornin'," he called as he heard her footsteps approaching the kitchen. "It's just me."

"This is a nice surprise." She leaned against the wall, barely in the kitchen, and smiled. "Haven't seen you around these parts for a while."

Guilt gutted him, but he put on a grin. "I know." He stepped away from the stove, where he was warming syrup, and gathered her into his arms. "I'm sorry I don't have time to treat you to breakfast every day." He kissed her forehead. "And lunch." He moved his lips to the tip of her nose. "And dinner." His mouth brushed her cheek. "And definitely dessert."

She met his kiss, and hope spiraled through him. Even if he only had time for one breakfast a week, he wanted to share it with her. She broke their connection and settled her cheek over his pulse.

"I'm sorry," he whispered into her hair. "I wish I had more time to spend with you." His fingers kneaded in tight circles along her lower back. "I'm sorry I treated you like a patient. I hate that you won't train Hank and Juniper."

"So you admit you think of me like a patient."

"I did," he said. "I don't anymore." He released her and poured the hot syrup into a serving jug. "Come on, let's eat."

He sat at the bar and dug into his French toast. "I'm sort of worried I haven't heard back from the bank. It's been over a week."

"I can call on Monday if you want," she said.

"Would you?"

"Of course."

"Maybe there's something else they need."

Chelsea swallowed and reached for her juice. "I don't think so."

"No?"

"Who do you think you're dealing with?" She grinned at him. "Those applications were flawless. I'll call on Monday." She jumped up. "Oh, that reminds me. I need you to sign some forms." She bustled out of the kitchen, leaving Pete to marvel at her willingness to help him, her easy forgiveness.

She returned to the kitchen carrying two folders. "This one is for the PATH International application. There were some things I didn't know because the program isn't fully operational yet, but I called their offices and they said to send it in anyway." She flipped open the folder and handed him a pen.

He signed his name and closed the folder, a new chapter in his life opening before him. One he could see himself doing, enjoying, every day. One that gave his life purpose.

"This one's for a federal grant for new startups that benefit veterans. And this one's a grant specifically for equine therapy programs."

He signed them both. "You should be a secretary," he said. "And a nurse. And a horse trainer. You're good at everything."

She beamed at him. "Good to know I have various skills." She tucked the pages into the folders and set them aside. "Is Reese coming tonight?"

"Yes," Pete said. "You should come. He's going to try riding, and it's his first time."

"I'll be there." She glanced around at the walls. "I've got to get out of here."

Pete understood the feeling. "Why don't we go to Amarillo today?" he suggested. "I'm open until this evening."

"Really?" Her eyes lit up and she pushed her half-eaten breakfast away. "I'll go shower right now." She practically pranced out of the kitchen.

Pete's pulse drummed in his eyes, his fingertips. Worry about that night's therapy session rose, filled him until he choked.

He put on a mask, one that allowed him to enjoy the drive to Amarillo with Chelsea tucked into his side. He enjoyed holding her hand as they walked around the mall and stopped for sandwiches.

"You're quiet today, sweetheart," he said over his Rueben.

"Just thinking of my friend," she said, pulling out her phone and checking it. "She just got engaged, and I've been thinking about her." She tucked the cell into her purse and then took a huge bite of her BLT. "I'll call her later."

"Getting engaged is bad?" he asked like he didn't care

about the answer.

"Jury's still out." Chelsea focused on him. "There's something magical about the city." She sighed into her palm as she rested her chin in her hand. "But there's nowhere like the ranch."

"So you're not a city slicker anymore." He wasn't really asking.

She grinned at him. "Depends on the company."

Pete's nerves disappeared, and they didn't return as long as Chelsea was with him. But by the time they'd driven back to Three Rivers and he'd changed into his work jeans, his stomach felt like it'd been gnawed by rats. As he exited his cabin, he heard the crunch of gravel under tires and hurried along the path between the calving stalls and the hay barn to the parking lot.

Chelsea hugged Reese, her face a beautiful balm to his worry. Pete stopped to watch her interact with the wounded veteran.

She grinned and tucked her arm in Reese's to help him into the barn. He couldn't hear what they said, but Reese laughed, his posture relaxed and his eyes dancing. *Chelsea could charm anyone*, Pete thought as he followed them.

"Hey," he said as he came up beside Reese. The man's limp was ten times worse than Squire's, as he'd lost a few inches due to a massive hip replacement. Consequentially, his abdomen muscle wall was weak. Equine therapy could improve the function of his hip, back, and abs.

"Pete." Reese shook his hand hello. "Chelsea just told me she'd be riding with me tonight."

Pete couldn't see Chelsea around Reese, and he was sure the surprise showed on his face. "She did?"

"Yes," she said, still not coming forward so Pete could read her face. "Hank misses me."

Pete chuckled. "I'm sure he does, sweetheart." He engaged Reese in talk about his job in Amarillo, his mother back in Arkansas, and how Reese was getting along in his new apartment.

"Things are hard," he said. "I tried to get a ground floor unit, but the only thing they had was on the third floor. It's veteran's housing, so I couldn't be too choosy. But man, it takes me forever to get up and down those stairs."

He spoke softly, hardly the commanding officer Pete knew he'd been. Coming home wounded took a lot out of someone, and admitting anything was hard landed a blow to already wounded pride.

"And I can't carry very much, because I'm using the railings. So it takes me several trips just to get groceries inside." Reese came to a stop outside Peony's pen, the horse already waiting for him.

"I can find someone to help with that," Chelsea said. "While I was researching some things for Pete, I saw some stuff on state-appointed care."

"Chelsea, he doesn't—" Pete started as Reese said, "I don't need extra care."

Chelsea's cheeks colored and she glanced between the

two men. "It's not like daycare," she said. "It's someone who gets paid to help you go get groceries, get to doctor's appointments, run your errands, that kind of thing." She gathered her hair into a ponytail, her words rushing. "It's nothing to be embarrassed about. They could do all your shopping for you, and carry everything in for you. It's a program designed to help wounded soldiers, not pity them."

Pete exchanged a glance with Reese. "Sounds like you could use an extra hand with groceries." He shrugged like he didn't care if Reese did or not. "Can't hurt to look into it."

"Probably not," Reese agreed.

"Great," Chelsea said. "I'll get you the information. Pete has your email?"

Reese nodded, his attention wandering to Peony. "So, we get to ride together," he said to her, his voice turning into putty as he petted the animal. "You ready for this?"

Pete squeezed Chelsea's fingers when he moved past her. "Let's get this horse saddled." He turned back to her. "You think you can handle Hank? Or do you want Peony?"

"Please," she scoffed. "Hank is the softest horse we have." She pivoted and started walking back to his stall, where he stood at the gate, his head over the railings, listening.

"Don't let him hear you say that!" Pete called after her, his heart growing warmer with every step she took.

Chapter Fourteen

Chelsea saddled Hank badly the first time, her mind far away on the conversation with Hailey. Scratch that. Hailey would've had to answer the phone in order for there to be a conversation. Worry wormed through Chelsea, but she pushed it away and focused on the horse.

With Pete's attention on Reese, she heaved the saddle off to readjust the blanket. "No need to go telling Pete about this," she said to Hank. "We can have our own secrets, you know."

The bay stallion nosed her thigh, somehow knowing exactly where her pocket was. "Yes, yes. I'll get you all the sugar cubes you want." She managed to get the blanket and saddle on the right way. She bridled him and led him to the back of the stall. "Wait here."

She hurried back to the gate and over to the tack room, where she grabbed a handful of sugar, the price of Hank's secrecy. She fed him one when she got back, and he nudged her chest the way he had last week.

"What?" she asked, but Hank just snuffled at her and hung his head while she raised the bar so they could move into the aisle.

They entered the arena first, and Chelsea used the fence to mount up. "Slow," she demanded as she took the reins in her hands. Hank's adrenaline buzzed through the air, infecting her.

"We're not in a race," she reminded him. "And Peony certainly won't want to run." She glanced toward the barn's opening without seeing Reese. "Reese is hurt. You let him go as slow as he wants, you hear?"

Hank tossed his head, and Chelsea gave him a pat on the neck. "Okay, fine. Run now. Get it all out." She loosened her grip on the reins, and the horse began to walk. Then trot and then gallop.

Hank only raced for a few minutes, then he slowed to a walk, his sides heaving and his head down.

"Here they are," she said as Reese emerged into the arena with Peony. She brought Hank to a stop while Pete instructed Reese. It took both of them to get him in the saddle, and Peony stood as still as a post the whole time.

Chelsea's core filled with love for her. For Hank. For these gentle horses who loved without restrictions. Without demands—well, except for the sugar cubes Hank adored.

"You ready?" Pete called to her. "Come on over here by Peony."

"Go on, Hank," she said. "You heard the man. Over by Peony."

Hank moved, circling around the other horse and alongside her.

"She'll go where he goes," he told Reese. "After a little while, we can remove him and you can start to take her where you want her."

Reese nodded, his face white and his grip on the reins much too tight. Chelsea reached over and put her hand on both of his. "It's okay," she said. "Trust them."

He lifted his eyes to hers and nodded.

"Okay, Hank. Take us out." The stallion moved the slowest she'd ever seen him, one hoof plodding in front of the next. The rhythm reminded her of Peony, who followed a head behind Hank.

Around they went, as Pete called instructions to Reese for where to put his hand, how to sit up taller, how to direct Peony. After several minutes, he said, "Okay, Chels, let's let them try on their own."

His face held worry in the lines around his mouth and the sharpness of his gaze. But his posture was relaxed; his hands hung between his knees.

Chelsea stopped Hank near the fence and turned to watch Reese take control in the arena. He maneuvered Peony like he'd been riding his whole life. His face glowed, his confidence skyrocketed.

Chelsea knew, because she felt everything he did as the emotions flitted across his face. After they'd finished, after Reese had left, after she'd fed Hank half his body weight in sugar, she sighed.

"That was incredible," she said to Pete as he tucked her against his side. "I see why this program means so much to you. Watching Reese...." She shook her head, unable to continue without getting choked up. "Incredible. You're really helping him."

"I'm not," Pete said. "Peony is."

"No." Chelsea stopped, pulling on Pete's hand to get him to stop too. Under the dark sky, with only faint light from the barn and the house, she studied his face. She wanted to memorize every crease of care, every angle, every line.

"No, it's you," she said. "You're the one training the horses to do what they do. You're the one with the passion for the program. You're the one getting people out here."

He shook his head, his movement slow, calculated. "Wrong again, sweetheart. You're the one who greeted Reese tonight. You're the one who trained Peony—and Hank. You're the one with the passion for the program." His face broke into a grin. "I'm just trying to keep up with you."

Her heart soared with her hopes as he kissed her. "See you in the mornin', sweetheart."

He'd called her sweetheart from the day they met. Then, it had been a name. Now, she felt the reverberations of emotion in the word. Now, the word sang through her soul, stitching together old hurts.

Now, it was an endearment.

* * *

MONDAY MORNING DAWNED with the promise of rain. Chelsea stood in the kitchen, nursing a cup of coffee, as she watched the wind blow leaves across the yard. Soon after, rain pelted the windows, solidifying her plans to stay inside. Her mother would've baked Halloween goodies for the cowhands. Chelsea had been banished from using the stove and oven, but she pulled out one of her mother's old cookbooks anyway. She thumbed through the pages, listening to the howling storm outside. At least it wasn't raging through her, the way it had at Danny's funeral.

Her phone chimed and she picked it up to see a text from Pete. *Lunch today?*

She considered going into town to buy something, but one look at the weather, and she vetoed that idea. *You forget I can't cook.*

Sandwiches, he messaged. *You have bread?*

Yes.

With a date set, she returned to her book browsing. By eleven-thirty, she had the bread and turkey out and started spreading mayonnaise. Her phone rang just as Pete burst through the French doors.

"Can you check that?" she asked over her shoulder.

He flung the raindrops from his hat and strode toward the counter where her phone continued to blare. "It's your brother." He answered it and switched on the speaker.

"Hello, Major," he said.

"Pete?" Squire's voice came through the phone. "Why are you answering my sister's phone?"

She met Pete's wide-eyed look with one of her own. "Hey, Squire," she called, her voice too loud.

"Chelsea." Squire lengthened her name the way her father used to when she was about to get in trouble. "Why is Pete Marshall answering your phone?"

"I'm making sandwiches." She laughed, but it sounded fake, fake, fake. "I'm up to my elbows in mayo." She'd actually put down the knife, their lunch forgotten.

"For the cowhands," her brother said.

She opened her mouth, but no air pushed past her vocal cords. Pete watched her with a devilish glint in his eyes.

"No," Pete said. "For me, Major. The cowhands know not to come to the homestead lookin' for food, what with that fire and all."

"Fire?" Squire's voice rose in pitch.

"It wasn't a fire," Chelsea said.

"There *was* a lot of smoke," Pete said.

"Shut up," she hissed. "The homestead is fine, Squire," she said louder. "Why are you calling?"

"I guess it's good you're both there. The bank called

me this morning about selling fifteen acres to Pete for his equine program."

Chelsea's heart pumped into overdrive as she hurried around the counter to where Pete held the phone. "Yeah?"

"I wanted to talk to you privately about it, but...."

"Squire," Chelsea said, locking eyes with Pete as she spoke. "Pete and I are seeing each other. I'd tell him whatever you said anyway."

"Seeing each other!" Squire's outburst didn't come across as a question, which brought a smile to Chelsea's face. "Chelsea—"

"I'm twenty-eight years old, Squire," she warned. "Pete's a good man."

"I know what kind of man my First Lieutenant is, Chelsea."

"Then you have no reason to be upset."

He sighed, and Chelsea heard the higher tone of Kelly in the background. She squeezed Pete's fingers, who'd turned to stone when she'd announced they were together.

"Okay," Squire said. "Kelly and I have talked about it, and I want to know what you think of gifting the land to Pete for Courage Reins. And the four horses he put in to buy."

"Gifting?" The word barely made it past her lips. She watched Pete. The vein in his neck throbbed and throbbed and throbbed.

"I think that's a great idea," Chelsea said. "We're applying for non-profit status as soon as we see about the construction loans and a couple of other things we're trying to get."

"Great," Squire said. "So I'll call the bank and let Miss Reyes know he doesn't need that loan. And I'll call Kevin and have him draw up the transfer of ownership papers."

"Thank you, Squire," Pete said, his voice set on frog mode.

"Pete? Can you take me off speaker?" Squire asked. "I want to talk to you without my nosy sister overhearing."

"Nosy?" Chelsea screeched, her insides shaking at the thought of what her Army Major brother needed to say to Pete that she couldn't hear.

Pete swiped the speaker off and held the phone to his ear. "Just me, Major."

"Okay, I don't know how to say this without just saying it, so I guess I'll say it. Chelsea's...."

"Strong?" Pete supplied, watching her worry her bottom lip between her teeth. "Kind? Organized? Helpful? Courageous? Pick one, Major."

"She's had a hard time lately."

Pete turned his back on her. "You mean when her fiancée died."

The silence coming through the line told Pete that Squire didn't think Chelsea had told him. "I know, Major. She's moving at the speed she can move at. So am I."

"And how fast is that, Pete?"

"Pretty slow."

Chelsea moved around him, her expression searching. "What's slow?"

"Nothing," he mouthed to her.

"Be careful with her, Lieutenant," Squire said. "Just... she's my sister, and I need you to be careful with her."

"You got it, Major."

Pete hung up and handed Chelsea her phone, twisting back to the half-assembled sandwiches. "I'm starving."

"You're starving?" She slammed the phone on the counter and picked up the knife. Pete decided teasing her with such a utensil in her hand wasn't a good idea.

"He's just worried about you," Pete said. "Wanted to make sure I wasn't pushing you to go too fast. Warned me against hurting you. You know, stuff brothers do for their sisters." He added a smile to his statement, hoping to soothe her mood.

She returned the gesture and layered turkey over the bread slices. "Overprotective man," she muttered.

Pete collapsed onto a barstool. "I can't believe he's gifting me the land. That's...." His throat closed with gratitude. Such a gesture was so Squire. Always giving, always looking out for his Army brothers.

Pete had shared a special bond with Squire since their first day in Afghanistan together. When the Major had carried Pete for over five miles because of an injury, their friendship had become lifelong. But gifting him fifteen acres of his family's ranch? That was beyond anything Pete had expected.

His phone rang, and he expected to have another man-to-man conversation with Squire about Chelsea. But the screen read Rose Reyes. "The bank," he said, and Chelsea dropped the knife again.

"Hello, Miss Reyes."

"Pete," she said. "How are you?"

"Great, great."

"I have some great news for you. Squire Ackerman has decided to gift you the acreage for Courage Reins. As well as the four horses. He's having his lawyer draw up the needed documentation. As for your construction loan, we have approved that, and the funds will be in your account by the end of the week. You can contact your contractor and get started."

Relief raged through Pete, dragging his shoulders down and expelling all the air from his lungs. "Thank you, Miss Reyes."

"I'm not done yet," she said, her words coated in joy. "The bank has generously gifted a large amount toward your project, so you will only be required to repay half of what you applied for."

"You're joking."

"What?" Chelsea demanded.

He shook his head, unable to put it in words yet.

"I never joke about money, Mister Marshall." Ms. Reyes laughed. "And Mari can't wait for her session tomorrow night. I'll see you then, and if you can't come into town before then, I'll bring the account information."

Pete thanked her again and hung up, staring unseeing at his phone. "The bank gifted us half the construction loan."

"Half?" Chelsea clutched her chest. "Pete, if we get those grants, you can start this business without a dime of debt."

Pete felt too full. Too full of gratitude. Too full of words. Too full of emotions. Too full of things that needed to be done.

"This is really happening," he said.

"You bet it is, Lieutenant," she said, sliding a plated turkey sandwich in front of him. "And I just made lunch without any issues, so today is a huge win for everyone." She sat next to him at the bar. "And you should make sure you include an island like this in your house."

"Oh yeah?" His eyebrows disappeared under the brim of his cowboy hat. "You plannin' on makin' me a lot of sandwiches, sweetheart?"

She nudged him with her shoulder, a beautiful blush coloring her face. "Maybe."

BRETT MURPHY, Pete's construction foreman, arrived a week later, a dark beard covering most of his face to match his thick hair.

Pete grinned as he shook his friend's hand and man-patted him on the shoulder. "Any trouble on the way in?"

Brett shook his head, his own smile seeming to be stuck in place. He took a deep, deep breath and glanced around the ranch. "Feels good to be here."

"Yeah," Pete agreed. "Three Rivers is a sanctuary."

Brett must've had sawdust in his veins, because he surveyed the land Pete had been given. "So walk me through it, Lieutenant."

"Okay, well, the homestead is going here." He turned and faced the Ackerman's house. He couldn't think of it as Chelsea's. "My front door will face theirs. And I need blue glass in the door."

"Blue glass?" Brett peered at him with a glint in his eye that Pete didn't like, didn't want to acknowledge.

"Yeah," Pete said in a falsely cheery tone. He clapped his hand on Brett's shoulder. "I have sketches back at my cabin, commander. You want to come see where you'll be livin'?"

Weeks later, the Halloween decorations had been replaced with turkeys and cornucopias. The ground for Courage Reins had been broken, with footings poured for the indoor arena, a small administration office, and Pete's homestead. The posts had been set for the pastures and grazing lots. Approval had come from one federal grant, which wasn't quite enough to cover the loan from the bank, but close.

Pete worked tirelessly on the ranch, moving from chore to chore like the zombie he'd become. He'd picked up two additional patients through Ms. Reyes, and with

Chelsea still training Hank and Juniper, Pete spent six nights a week working with the equine therapy program.

He needed volunteers to oversee the sessions. Volunteers to make appointments. A volunteer to create a website. The to-do list went on and on.

He managed to carve out a Saturday morning breakfast with Chelsea every week, and though she didn't complain about his twenty-four-seven schedule, he noticed new distance between them. He simply didn't have any more to give her. Breakfast on Saturday and his undivided attention for church and the Sunday picnic would have to be enough for now.

Brett worked all day on the construction of Courage Reins, and often he and Pete would walk through the plans, or the physical space where the house was being built.

Brett had taken over the bunk Squire had vacated, and Pete spent time picking up mangy boots and washing twice as many dishes.

"I'm not your maid or your mother," Pete told him a few days before Thanksgiving. "You've got to put away your own stuff."

Brett lounged on the couch at mid-day, as the rain had stalled the progress on Pete's house. The frame had gone up last week, but the skeleton had no roof and no solid walls.

"Okay," Brett said, but Pete had chastised him last

week, and nothing had changed. He scrubbed out his frustration on the pan he'd used to make lunch.

"Do we need to re-draw the laundry room?" Pete asked, pulling out the sketches Brett then turned into blueprints.

"If you want that stacked unit, it should be fine. I'll just make the counter longer for Chelsea." He seized, his foot slipping from the coffee table to thunk on the floor. "I mean—"

"I do my own laundry," Pete said, his voice as dark as a raven's wing. "And yours."

"Yeah, and thank you," Brett said quickly.

Pete remained silent, Brett's words sprinting through his head. So his efforts to design his house for Chelsea hadn't gone unnoticed. He shouldn't be surprised. Brett had always been observant, and thoughtful, and when he spoke, Pete usually needed to listen. He stared at the back of Brett's dark-haired head, trying to worm his way inside his thoughts. Did he think it a good thing or a bad thing Pete imagined living in his homestead with Chelsea?

Pete had never pictured a life with a woman at all, which made his laundry-friendly designs all the more confusing.

"I have to get back to work," Pete said, eyeing the plate sitting next to Brett. "Put that in the dishwasher."

"You got it, boss."

Pete shook his head as he left his cabin. Brett could probably benefit from the equine program, but Pete could barely keep up with the few clients he had. Brett didn't have physical wounds, but Pete knew what kinds of things he'd seen overseas. And those things couldn't be unseen, unfelt, undone. They could be healed, though, and Pete whistled a tune as he opened the door to the admin trailer.

Tom's desk sat empty, not completely unusual. Pete headed to the cowhand's area, where the white board listed the day's assignments. The box next to his name was blank, and Pete frowned. All the boxes were blank. Pete wondered if the weather had cancelled work for the day, or if the winter season just didn't support full-day workloads.

He glanced toward the offices, but Garth's was dark and empty. The entire trailer was empty. A slithery chill slipped up Pete's neck. His scalp prickled.

Something was wrong. He headed back outside, pausing under the roof to stay out of the rain. The usual ranch trucks were parked to his right. The horse barn was open, and the wind muted the normal sounds of chickens squawking and cattle lowing.

He returned to Tom's desk and picked up the radio there. "Pete here. You there, Tom?"

No answer. Pete felt like he was falling for a moment, his stomach swooping down and then up.

He gripped the radio as he left the trailer and headed to the horse barn. The silence screamed at him, reminding him of an assignment required of every cowhand: Moving the herd.

All the horses were gone.

Pete leaned against the doorway for support. He'd forgotten. Forgotten because of the rain. Forgotten because he'd missed the morning meeting and had checked the board a few minutes late. Forgotten because Brett had found him just before lunch and they'd gone back to the cabin together, talking about dimensions and paint colors and flooring options.

Simply forgotten.

The boys could only be an hour ahead of him. He could catch up. Maybe no one would realize he hadn't been there from the beginning.

If only he had a horse. He hurried down the aisle toward Hank's stall. But he'd been taken, even though the ranch didn't own him anymore. Pete's frustration frothed, mixing with anger and confusion. Garth had no right to take Peony, or Hank, or Juniper, or Baywatch.

He spun, intending to find someone and figure out what was going on, where the relocation party was headed.

Garth stood in the doorway. "You missed the boys," he called. "They left a while ago."

Pete strode toward him, his jaw working as he tamped down his temper. "Did you take my horses?" He swept his hand toward all the empty stalls. "They're not working horses."

Garth bristled, his anger obvious to Pete. He hadn't been happy about the paperwork stating that Pete owned those four horses, but he'd accepted it. Filed a copy in his office and warned Pete to keep up with his work on the ranch.

"Your horses are in the hay barn," Garth said. "Pete, this was a mandatory trip. Everyone knew they'd be gone until Wednesday, and then they'd get the Thanksgiving weekend off."

Pete shoved his hands in his pockets. "I know. I was planning to go."

Garth cocked his eyebrow. "So what happened?"

"I forgot." The words sounded so weak, so much like an irresponsible teenager.

"Pete, this isn't a job you get to forget about."

Pete exhaled, that anger-frustration concoction back in his blood. "I know that, sir. My contractor—"

Garth held up his hand to cut Pete off. "I don't really need to know the details. I'm afraid all your work with the equine program—which I'm in favor of, to be clear—has interfered with your ranch responsibilities."

Pete dropped his eyes to the dirt, shame shushing the anger. "It won't happen again."

"No, it won't."

Panic joined the emotional cocktail churning in Pete's gut. "Sir?"

"It's time to make a choice, son." Garth spoke in a calm tone, almost apologetic. He lifted his cowboy hat and ran his fingers through his dark hair salted with gray though Garth couldn't be over forty.

Pete had a flash of his father, of his patience, of his unwillingness to bend on certain points. Like keeping his room neat, helping his momma, and taking care of the horses at their boarding stable. Garth wasn't nearly as old as Pete's dad would've been, but he felt very much like he'd disappointed someone he never wanted to hurt.

"You can't do the equine program and keep your job here." Garth watched him with concern in his gaze. "I see how tired you are."

Pete's mind raced. If he quit on the ranch, he didn't have much of an income. He was still working out the administrative policies of Courage Reins, which included his benefits and salary the non-profit organization would pay.

He did get a small wage from his time in the Army. Maybe enough to squeak by until he could get the finances of Courage Reins in order. Ms. Reyes had said to keep his inheritance for a rainy day, and today felt like a monsoon.

"Pete?"

"So you're saying I have to quit or be fired?"

"I'm saying you need to choose one job. Having both of these isn't healthy."

"I choose Courage Reins."

Garth gave a single nod, his brown eyes full of understanding. Maybe even approval. "I'll give you a severance package through the end of the year."

Tar coated Pete's soft places inside. He loved Three Rivers Ranch. Had felt accepted here, among cowboys and ranchers. Had found peace here among horses and cows and chickens. Sadness infiltrated his senses, painting the rainy day in darker drips of gray.

"I'll get Tom on the paperwork after Thanksgiving," Garth said. "And Pete, you'll have to vacate the cabin. Brett too. I'll need it for a new cowhand."

Ice shards spread down Pete's legs as Garth walked away. No job. Nowhere to live. Nothing to offer Chelsea.

He sighed, the sound joining the whipping of the wind and the pounding of rain. He felt the weather in his soul, chilling him, taunting him, driving him mad.

But Courage Reins meant too much to him to abandon now. If only he knew the next step, could see that in a year, things would be better. Heck, he'd take next week being better than this one.

He remembered something Squire had said to him when he'd first arrived on the ranch. *Let God guide you.*

Lord, he prayed. *If there ever was a time where I needed guidance, it's now.*

The world stilled, just for a beat, a breath. The rain paused, the wind silenced, the frenzied thoughts in Pete's mind fled.

Life rushed forward again, but in that one moment, that single inhalation, Pete had felt God's presence.

Be still, and know that I am God.

Pete knew. He might not know where to go next, or what would happen, or how things would fall into place. But he knew they would.

* * *

"So we have to move out?" Brett glanced around the cowboy cabin like it was the Taj Mahal and he'd personally decorated it.

Pete scrubbed the back of his neck and studied the floor. He'd only been in the cabin for several months, but it felt more like home than anywhere he'd stayed since he'd been discharged. Since his momma's and granddad's deaths.

"Listen," he said. "I'm sure you can stay with Chelsea."

Brett's eyebrows shot up, getting swallowed by the brim of his cowboy hat, but Pete plowed on. "She has a huge house. The basement is empty."

"You talk to her about it?"

"Not yet." Pete abandoned his Lieutenant skin and collapsed on the couch. He pressed his fists into his eye sockets. Telling Chelsea he'd lost his job and had nowhere to live ranked dead last on his list of things he wanted to do.

"But I'm sure it'll be fine." He glanced at Brett.

"You gonna live there with her?" Brett folded his arms like he already knew the answer.

"No," Pete said.

"Hmm." Brett adjusted his hat. "Well, I guess I better go talk to her. If you want the construction to stay on schedule, I can't be drivin' in from Oklahoma

City on weekends." He put one hand on the doorknob.

Pete's mind whirred, writhed, as he tried to come up with a solution for himself. Maybe Heidi and Frank would let him stay with them in their condo. But then they'd ask why he couldn't bunk in the basement....

"You comin' or what?" Brett barked, pulling Pete from his dilemma.

"Yeah, I'm comin'." He exhaled heavily as he got to his feet. With every step closer to spilling his guts to Chelsea, Pete prayed for the right words.

Chapter Fifteen

"You can move into my basement," Chelsea said. She'd said it yesterday too. And the day before that, when Pete and Brett had shown up in her kitchen dripping wet to say Pete had quit his job and they couldn't stay in the cowboy cabin. "It's Thanksgiving tomorrow, and I already have all the food." She slid him a sly smile. "I just need a handsome chef to cook it."

"I'll be here early to get started on the turkey," Pete said. "Brett's eating with us. We don't have to move until next week—Garth's being cool about the whole thing—but I am *not* moving in with you."

Chelsea understood his reasons why, but on an emotional level, she wanted to help him. "What will the neighbors think?"

"Chelsea," Pete warned.

"Oh, come on." She tucked her hand into his and

snuggled into him. Since he hadn't been working during the day, he'd taken to joining her about midmorning after he'd been to the construction site and been brought up to speed on the progress by Brett.

A movie played on the TV in front of them, and if the past two days predicted a pattern—and with Pete they did —he'd make her lunch before he headed over to the barn to putter around with the horses. Chelsea admitted that she liked him better after he returned from brushing Peony, or riding Baywatch, or simply feeding sugar cubes to Hank. The horses worked their equine magic on Pete as well as anyone else, though she'd never told him as much.

"Kelly and Squire are coming for Christmas," she told Pete. "Kelly said she'd help with the cooking so you don't have to do it all."

"Sounds fantastic," Pete said, lifting his arm and securing Chelsea against his side. "Can we take a nap now, sweetheart?"

She giggled as she wrapped her arm across his waist. "You do that, cowboy."

And he did. As his chest rose and fell, Chelsea's worry ebbed in and out too. He wasn't acting like himself. At least not the Pete Marshall she'd met and known for the past six weeks. That man didn't sleep in the middle of the day. He didn't glower. He didn't need the horses to heal him.

Or maybe he had, and she hadn't noticed because

she'd been so warped. But her heart was almost straight now, her mind much quieter.

The cowhands would be back from moving the herd today, and Chelsea had invited them all to the house for dinner. She had to drive into town to pick up the food that afternoon. She'd also told Garth that anyone who didn't have somewhere to go for Thanksgiving was welcome at the homestead. With Pete cooking, they'd have a traditional feast.

Her phone chimed, and she eased out of Pete's arms to retrieve it. She'd received an email, and her heartbeat jumped to the moon when she saw it was from PATH International. She closed her eyes and drew a deep breath.

The email had already been typed. God couldn't change that, but Chelsea prayed anyway. *Please be good news.*

She couldn't read fast enough. *Thanks for applying, blah blah blah, your application to PATH International has been approved.*

"Yes!" Chelsea covered her mouth when she realized she'd shouted. But Pete hadn't moved. Getting into PATH meant their facility would be listed on the organization's website. They'd advertise to veterans that Courage Reins existed. This was a huge marketing win.

She closed her email and opened her electronic to-do list. She deleted *Join PATH International*, and added *Design a website for Courage Reins*. With her marketing background, she knew a professional and easy-to-use website would go a long way.

There was another equine therapy program in Amarillo, and to get people to come to Three Rivers instead of going there would require good marketing. Chelsea had designed websites for high-profile clients and done social media consulting as a regular part of her job in Dallas.

"Courage Reins is going to have the best website on the planet," she vowed, closing her to-do list and focusing on a still-sleeping Pete. With his features relaxed, she saw the man she cared so much about.

Something sparked in her stomach. She cared a *lot* about that man.

Before she could wax emotional, her phone sounded again. This time, it was a text from Hailey.

Broke up with Rob. Thought you'd want to know.

Chelsea's thumb hovered over the call button, but she didn't press it. Relief spread through her that Hailey didn't have to go through the same pain, the same suffering, she had.

Are you happy? she texted.

Happier now came the response. If there was anything Chelsea understood, it was that.

* * *

"Hey, Mom," Chelsea called as she entered her parent's condo.

"Chelsea." She bustled out of the kitchen, wiping her hands on her apron. Smudges of flour marred the fabric. "How are you, dear?"

Chelsea relaxed into her mother's hug, breathing deeply to take strength from her. "I'm doing good, Mom. So much better."

Her mother held her at arm's length. "I'm so glad, baby." She wiped her powdery fingers down Chelsea's cheek. "I'm in the middle of a batch of rolls. Come in the kitchen."

Every available surface in the kitchen held bread. Crescent rolls. Dinner rolls. Parker House rolls. Clover-leaf rolls, one of which Chelsea plucked from a still-warm muffin tin and pinched off one of the three nubs. She groaned at the buttery, light texture.

"Mom, you're a genius. How is it that I can't even boil water?"

As usual, her mother simply smiled. "I'm bringing all these to the ranch tomorrow. Did you figure out how many boys will be there?"

"I talked to Garth just before I left," Chelsea said. "I think there will be about fifteen of us. Plus you and Dad." She took in the dozens and dozens of rolls. "I think you have too many rolls, Mom."

"They freeze," her mom said. "And you can take some for dinner tonight. The boys are hungry after they move the herd."

Chelsea's chest squeezed. "I wish I could cook," she

said. "You made a family with those cowhands, and that's changed." Sadness colored her words. She wanted the cowboys to feel part of something at Three Rivers. Her mom had always done that, made her home theirs, opened her life to them. The easiest way to do that was through food, and Chelsea simply didn't have the skill.

Her mom cleared her throat and kneaded the bread dough extra hard.

"What is it, Mom?"

"I can teach you to cook." She kept her eyes on the counter. "It can't take you long to keep up the house, and I'm lonely here without people to cook for or a big house and yard to take care of." She shrugged like her loneliness didn't impact Chelsea, but a pinch had started at the back of her throat.

"I can come in the afternoons," Chelsea said. "I might even have a friend who might want to come with me." She thought of Ruby, and if she really did want to take cooking classes.

Her mother looked up, her eyes glassy and wide. "That would be wonderful." She sniffed as a smile broke her face in half. "We can start with boiling water."

Chelsea laughed and stood. "Well, I need to get the food back to the ranch before it gets too cold. Help me carry out the rolls you're donating for tonight?"

With her SUV full of the delicious smells of roasted meat and cheesy potatoes—and at least five dozen baked goods from her mother—Chelsea sang along with the radio. The sky held the hint of another storm, but it wouldn't arrive for a few hours. As of now, the world was peaceful, matching the energy floating through Chelsea.

Pete met her in the garage. "The boys got back twenty minutes ago. They're showering and heading over."

"Great. Help me get this stuff in and set up." She lifted two huge pans of mashed potatoes, bending under their weight.

The cheery light reminded her of the childhood home she'd loved. Pete had set out plates and silverware, lit lanterns on the deck, and set up four long folding tables with chairs.

"You've been busy," she said to Pete as he set a vat of green salad next to the potatoes. "Thank you so much."

"Anytime, sweetheart." He stole a kiss before straightening his hat. "How's your momma?"

"She's good. Lonely. She's going to teach me to cook."

Pete paused near the mudroom, where he'd been heading to get another load of food. "She is?"

"Yes." Chelsea stepped past him. "I want this place to be as magical as I remember it. I want the boys to come up to the house for breakfast, or lunch, or dinner. I want to give them that family atmosphere my mom was so good at. That starts with food."

Admiration shone in Pete's eyes, along with something hotter. He kissed her again, this time with the care and precision of that first kiss by the stream. This time with the slow passion burning through her core.

When he stepped back, she fell forward, like she couldn't stand without his assistance.

"I adore you," he said before ducking through the mudroom and into the garage.

Chelsea stood statuesque, her fingertips brushing against her lips. She wasn't sure if *I adore you* meant the same thing as three other words. But it was easy to translate it to *I love you*.

Pete banged through the door, breaking the spell surrounding Chelsea. "All that's left is the bread," he said.

"I'll get it." She hurried down the steps, emotion filling her to overflowing. "He adores me," she whispered to herself, a smile stealing across her face as she loaded her hands with her mom's baking.

She adored him too.

Monday morning came, as Monday mornings always did. Pete woke, and his first thought was *moving day*.

Brett had gladly accepted Chelsea's invitation to take over her basement, but Pete absolutely could not. Not only would propriety not allow it, but he couldn't imagine telling Squire he was now living with his sister.

He'd set up a tent in the backyard of his homestead, on the side away from the ranch. Brett had promised to accelerate the construction on the house so Pete wouldn't have to rough it for too long, but December loomed only days away and it wasn't exactly warm.

He hauled his two Army duffle bags to his new home, set up his cot, and stacked bottled water against the leeward side to brace the tent against the wind.

Brett helped Pete clean the cabin, and Pete headed to Garth's office to turn over the key.

"All out," Pete said. "Thank you for everything."

"Let me know if you need anything." Garth flipped the key around in his fingers. "Hot shower. Hot meal."

"Brett moved into the homestead's basement. I'm going to be showering there. Chelsea said I can use her kitchen."

Garth nodded. "I'm looking forward to working with you on the therapeutic program."

Pete's throat closed, so he nodded and left the administration trailer. Tom wasn't at his desk, which probably helped Pete avoid another awkward goodbye.

And it wasn't really goodbye. His homestead lay a hundred yards south of the trailer. He'd still be working in the horse barn and arenas. He wasn't really leaving Three Rivers. The thought lightened his mood and bounced his step.

* * *

BRETT WASTED no time putting Pete to work. His first task: A list of items they needed from the hardware store.

"And then you're gonna help me build this house." Brett had wielded a sharp twinkle in his eye when he spoke, and Pete knew he was about to be schooled in the art of construction.

He put hammers and nails, tar paper and tiles, in the cart. He ordered the flooring Brett had specified. Unloaded one cart into his truck and went back for painting supplies. As he left the store for the second time, he caught sight of Reese wheeling his way into the deli next door.

"Reese!"

The wheelchair turned and Reese peered toward Pete. "Oh, hey." He lifted his hand in a wave.

"You eatin'?" Pete asked.

"Yeah. You want to join me?"

"Let me unload this paint, and I'll be right there."

Ten minutes later, Pete sat across from Reese with a hefty club sandwich and a tall soda. He took a long drink and sighed.

"How's things?" he asked Reese.

"Good enough." He glanced at his lap. "I use the wheelchair when I'm especially tired."

Pete nodded, not sure what to say. He hadn't known Reese needed a wheelchair, even sporadically.

"You find out about that care program?" Pete tried not to employ his Lieutenant voice, but he didn't quite pull it off.

Reese chuckled. "Four minutes. It only took you four minutes to go commanding officer on me."

Pete's gut pinched, but he didn't back down. "I could have Chelsea call you every day until you do it."

Reese wiped his mouth. "As least I'd have a pretty voice naggin' me."

A flush worked its way up Pete's neck. "She misses you. When you comin' back out for a ride?"

"When she asks me."

Pete grinned at his friend. "Expect a call later today. And I'll make sure she nags you about the care program too."

Reese finished his sandwich and ripped open his bag of potato chips. "No need, Lieutenant Marshall. I'm meeting my coordinator here in...." He checked his cell. "Five minutes."

"You're meeting here?" Pete glanced around like he'd forgotten where they were. "But you live in Amarillo."

"I'm movin' here." Reese's chest puffed out and a grin pulled against the corners of his mouth. "I like it here. It's quieter. More peaceful. Less stress. Plus, it's closer to the facility." He filled his mouth with chips, the conversation clearly over.

"That's great," Pete said. "When are you moving?"

"Next weekend."

"I'll come help. I have another Army buddy in town building my facilities out on the ranch. He'll come too."

Reese shook his head. "Not needed. My veteran care coordinator is handling it all."

Pete's eyebrows rose as a vein of happiness infused his heart. Reese looked good. "And you haven't met him yet?"

"Her." A voice said from beside their table.

Pete and Reese looked up in unison. Pete took in the clearly feminine form standing there, her auburn hair tucked neatly into a braid and her charcoal pantsuit clearly tailored to fit her exact dimensions.

"You must be Reese." Her smile could've melted ice cream as she extended her hand to Reese.

"Yes, ma'am." He exchanged a glance with Pete. "But my coordinator is Lex."

"Alexis Bright, at your service." Her green eyes sparked with challenge and life. Pete liked her. "And if you call me ma'am again, soldier, I might have to tamper with the brakes on your chair."

She laughed, and Pete decided he liked her a lot. One look at Reese, and Pete knew he did too.

"Now." She pulled a chair over and placed a folder on top of Reese's sandwich wrapper. "Here's the condo we got for you. Ground unit. Everything is set for next weekend."

Reese flipped through a few pages, his fingers shaking the tiniest bit. Pete tried to get a read on Lex, but she kept her attention on Reese.

"Looks good?" she asked.

"Yes." Reese cleared his throat before locking eyes

with Pete. "Tell Chelsea she doesn't need to call. I'll be out to ride tomorrow night, if that's okay."

With Reese's eyes shining like glass, and Pete's voice all tangled with the emotion gathering in his throat, all Pete could do was nod.

* * *

A WEEK LATER, the house had a roof and walls that would keep out the wind and rain. Brett was a construction foreman through and through, driving Pete from the break of dawn until past dusk. Pete had become quite adept at hammering instead of shoveling, and together they'd made huge strides in the construction.

A good thing, because a winter storm blew through the Texas Panhandle on Saturday night, driving Pete from his tent and into the simple structure. Without heat and electricity, all he had was relief from the rain.

He couldn't stay here, but he worried he might not make it to Garth's in the pitch blackness.

"Pete!" Chelsea's high voice cut through the shrieking of the wind.

He hurried to the back door and down the steps, the rain driving through his clothes. "Chelsea! What are you doing out here?"

She fell into his arms, soaking wet and shivering despite her heavy coat. "Looking for you. You can't stay out here. Please come into the house."

With little choice, he wrapped his arm around her and they fought their way to the homestead. They burst into the warm, bright sanctuary of the kitchen, panting and dripping.

"You didn't need to come for me," he said. "I have a phone."

"You didn't answer it," she said, peeling off her coat. Her pajamas stuck to every curve of her body, and Pete dropped his eyes to the floor.

He felt his pockets for the phone, but didn't find it. "I must've dropped it or left it in the tent."

"You can't keep living in that tent." She snatched a blanket from the couch and wrapped it around herself. "There's plenty of room in the basement, and it has a separate entrance. We would *not* be living together."

Pete exhaled, already tired of this argument though she'd let it drop for the past several days. He heard a new edge in her voice now, though, one that would not be ignored.

"That's the tip of the iceberg, sweetheart," Pete said.

She widened her eyes. "Tell me the rest, then."

Pete shrugged out of his sopping coat, and then his denim shirt so that he only wore his tank top. It was wet too, and he shivered. "I don't think so."

She handed him a blanket, and he set it across his shoulders. "So you don't want to share your life with me." She sounded like a wounded animal, small and shivery.

"Of course I do."

"Then tell me."

"I don't want to depend on you," he said. "*I* want to provide a good life for *you*. And what do I have? A construction debt and a tent." He pressed his lips together, determined not to say anything more. She could see his inadequacies. Everyone could. He didn't need to spell them out.

"Pete, you're all I need."

"Come on, sweetheart," he bit the words out. "We both know that's not true." He swept his arm around the room. "Look at this place. It's wonderful, and you're not happy here."

Tears filled her eyes. "That's completely unfair. My happiness has nothing to do with my physical surroundings."

"Right." Pete laughed. "So you want to sleep on my cot in my tent? I don't think so."

"I just want to be with you." She blinked the water away. "Because I love you."

Her words slammed into his chest, crashed through his ribs, exploded in his heart. The lights in the kitchen seemed to brown out and then come back to life twice as blinding as before.

She loved him.

"I love you Lieutenant Marshall, and I want you to be happy." Her words released the dam in his throat. "But I know I can't *make* you happy."

"I *am* happy. But I have so much going on, and I can't

provide you with the life you deserve." Why couldn't she see that? "I can't depend on your money, your inheritance. I have to make my own way in this world."

"Why? It won't be forever, and I don't care if it is."

"Because!" The band constricting his chest broke, snapped, shattered. "Because I watched my momma support us by herself after my daddy died overseas. It was hard for her. She cried at night sometimes, worked two jobs, raised me by herself." His chest heaved as his memories crowded out of the box he kept them in.

"Growing up, she used to tell me to get a good job, find a good woman, and take good care of her. I promised her I would." He took a step closer, sucking, sucking, sucking at the air. "I can't break that promise. You're the best woman I've ever had in my life, but I'm working as hard as I know how to find a way to keep that promise."

His anger faded at the trembling of her lower lip. "I adore you," he said. "I *love* you. I want you in my life for always." He took a step closer to her, everything in him itching to hold her, kiss her, ask her to be his. "But I will not depend on you, not even for one day."

She nodded, tears splashing her cheeks. "Bad timing."

He swiped his fingers across her face, stealing her tears and wishing he could erase them. "The worst."

"So you're choosing Courage Reins over me." She lifted her eyes to his, a measure of challenge in her gaze he'd never seen before.

"Chelsea." A dose of defeat doused with exasperation

tainted his voice. If that was what she wanted to believe....

"Yes. Right now, I'm choosing Courage Reins over you."

* * *

PETE ESCAPED the basement before the dawn could fully chase away the darkness. Thankfully, the storm had blown itself out during the night. At least the physical clouds that dropped rain. The raging tempest in Pete's chest had spread to every extremity, darkened every corner of his mind.

He couldn't erase the look of hurt from Chelsea's face. The way her lower lip shook. The tight clench of her arms around her stomach, like she was trying not to let herself shatter in front of him.

He trudged down the path in front of the cowboy cabins, keeping his gaze fixed on the largest one the farthest from the homestead but closest to the admin trailer. Garth's cabin.

Thinking it too early to knock, Pete crashed into a deck chair on the porch, his fingers itching to find something he could smash. Instead, he closed his eyes and leaned back, hoping the calm morning would infuse some relief into his bloodstream.

"You lost?" Garth's voice startled Pete's heart into a gallop.

Pete cleared his throat as he stood to look Garth in the eye. "Wonder if I might take you up on your offer of a shower." He raised his chin. "Sir," he added as an afterthought.

Garth squinted into the distance. Pete didn't want to know what he was thinking, what he'd heard about Pete and Chelsea.

"Sure, Pete." He hooked his thumb toward the door. "I have coffee on too."

Relief flowed through Pete like white water rapids, pouring and splashing all the way down to his feet. "Thanks, Garth. Coffee sounds great." He followed the foreman into the cabin, grateful for small miracles.

"I've got burgers on the menu for tonight," Garth said as he stuck two slices of bread in the toaster. "You're welcome to have one."

Later that evening, Pete headed over to Garth's cabin about six to help make dinner. Brett blocked his exit from the roughed out living room. "You don't need to stay away from the homestead."

"I'm not avoiding the homestead," Pete lied. "Chelsea surely didn't make dinner anyway."

"Pete—"

"You could come to Garth's, I'm sure." Pete's voice sounded like glass in the garbage disposal.

Brett's shoulders fell; his mouth tightened into a fierce line.

"No? Okay, well, I'll see you tomorrow." He stepped around Brett and continued to Garth's.

Over the next couple of weeks, Pete traded chores like

laundry and dishes for a good cut of steak and a hot shower.

But Garth was poor company compared to Chelsea.

She stopped texting him updates on the grants she found online. He took over finding volunteers, and even managed to hire a psychologist to come from Amarillo to the ranch twice a week for his patients.

A week before Christmas, he slathered a coat of gray paint on the living room walls while Brett measured something in the kitchen. Pete's thoughts circled Chelsea and if she'd like the shade he'd chosen.

Brett began installing the custom cabinets Pete had designed. He'd made the layout easy and user-friendly as Chelsea was still learning to cook. He'd included an island, as she'd mentioned once that he should have one in his house. He wouldn't think about her standing there, making him a turkey sandwich while her brother warned him about hurting her.

He managed to banish the thoughts for five seconds before everything about the house screamed Chelsea, and fury roared through him like a thunderstorm. He threw the paintbrush to the floor and stalked toward the back exit—French doors like what Chelsea was used to off her kitchen.

French doors she'd probably never use. French doors she didn't care about.

"Hey, where you—?" Brett asked before Pete tossed him a glare and stepped onto the deck. He didn't have a walk-out basement like the Ackerman's. His homestead wasn't on a swell, and he'd designed a two-story structure instead. A place large enough for him and Chelsea to raise a family together.

He pushed his anger out through his footsteps, arriving at the skeleton of the indoor training facility in just a few minutes. Horse stalls lined the back of the structure, with an open area to work with the horses in the front when the weather was bad. Pete had read about the best way to synthesize the dirt found in an outdoor arena, and he'd contacted a rubber stamp company in Utah for their ends. They'd agreed to the donation yesterday.

"Who cares?" he bellowed into the sky. "Who cares if the indoor arena will be gentle on the horse's hooves? Who cares if the house is big enough for a family?" His fists clenched and energy surged from his feet to his brain.

"I don't care!"

"Yes, you do." Brett's calm voice behind him didn't ease the pain pouring through Pete. Even being burned alive hadn't hurt like losing Chelsea. All the skin grafts, the shots the nurses loved to give him, the deaths of his momma and granddad. Nothing seared like losing Chelsea.

"You care about this program, and you care about that woman."

"Brett," Pete warned. "Don't."

"I live in her basement. You think I haven't seen what's gone on?"

Pete turned away from the half-built arena. "What have you seen?"

Brett shrugged like he hadn't seen anything of importance. The commander didn't quite pull it off.

"I outrank you," Pete said. "You better start talkin'."

Laughter sprang from Brett's mouth, which only irritated Pete further. "Always back to the Army."

"The Army runs in my blood," Pete said. "Did you know I actually consider you lucky that you get to keep serving?" He sighed and turned away again. "I was career Army, like my dad. Only thing I ever wanted—to be like him. Even my momma couldn't keep me from joining up."

"But this is so much more suited to you," Brett said. "I've seen you with those horses. It's incredible."

"What have you seen at Chelsea's?"

"Let's just say that I didn't know a person could cry that much."

Helplessness snagged in Pete's lungs, making him lean against the arena wall and gasp, gasp, gasp for air.

"It's obvious you're meant for each other," Brett said. "So what's the problem?"

Pete spun back to his house, two stories tall and proud. Brett had a brick mason coming the first week of January, and the electricity would be activated that same week.

"I chose my equine program over her," Pete finally said.

"I know you built that house for her," Brett said. "Men

don't care about in-floor heating in the master bath." He crossed his arms and cocked his eyebrows.

"So what if I did?"

"Go talk to her."

"When the facilities are done. When Courage Reins is off the ground."

"Lieutenant," Brett said. "That's at least another six months out."

Six months. Six months of this hurt, this razor blade in his chest. He could survive six more months.

Who was he kidding? No way he'd make it six more months without Chelsea.

Chapter Sixteen

"Gently," Chelsea's mom coached as Ruby began folding egg whites into the Belgian waffle batter. "We spent all that time getting air into them, we don't want to smash it out."

"Gently, got it," Ruby repeated. Chelsea watched from across the counter, her own egg whites beating in the stand mixer.

"You want your pans waiting for you," her mother said next. "So that's why we plugged in the waffle iron before we measured the flour. It's never good to have wet ingredients mixed with dry and then have your oven or pan too cold."

"Pre-heat," Chelsea said. "Check."

Ruby's baby, Porter, began to fuss. He kicked his legs, sending the swing she'd strapped him into flailing.

"Can you grab him?" Ruby glanced at Chelsea, a panicked edge in her eyes. "My batter is almost done."

Chelsea, who hadn't yet mixed her wet ingredients with her dry, took a step toward the ten-month-old. She fumbled with the buckle, not quite sure how to get it to release. Porter kicked and howled at her, baby-talk for "hurry up!"

"I'm trying," she muttered just as she managed to release the clasp. She lifted the squirming baby into her arms, glad when he settled down. "There you go." She bumped the cutie pie with her hip and tickled his neck.

He squealed and buried his face in her shoulder. A strong sensation of longing almost sent Chelsea to her knees. She'd only had Squire for a sibling, and they were so close in age, she'd never taken care of him.

And she realized, standing in her mother's cramped condo kitchen, with Ruby getting a lesson on how to fill a waffle iron, that she wanted children. She ran her fingers through Porter's fine, brown hair and imagined a baby with Pete's sandy hair and striking green eyes.

Her heart seized, stuttered, stalled. The world narrowed to the three feet surrounding Chelsea, but she fought back the panic. She'd vowed not to wear an engagement ring for a third time. How could she be fantasizing about having children with Pete?

To have a baby, there'd need to be a wedding first. Her chest tightened, her lungs squeezed, her left ring finger felt like someone had pressed a branding iron to it.

"Chelsea?" Her mother's steady voice, her warm touch, brought Chelsea away from the edge of reason.

"I'll take him." She reached for the baby. "Your egg whites are ready." Her mother gave her a knowing look before placing a gentle kiss on Porter's head.

"How's Pete?"

Chelsea ducked her head and scampered back to the counter where her bowl of flour, sugar, salt, and baking powder waited. "He's fine," she managed to push out through a too-dry throat.

"Mmm hmm." Her mother stepped next to her.

"Mom, drop it." Chelsea hadn't told Ruby about her relationship with Pete, and thus hadn't needed to disclose anything about their breakup. She was surprised her mother knew, but knowing Pete, he'd probably come clean within an hour of their disastrous conversation and subsequent break-up.

"Drop what?" Ruby asked, alarmed. "What did I do wrong?" She glanced at her steaming waffle iron and then the floor.

"Nothing, hon," Chelsea's mom said. "You're doing just fine."

* * *

THE FOLLOWING WEEK, Chelsea wandered down Main Street, Christmas gifts on her mind. She'd been planning an all-out feast at the homestead. Any cowhand that wasn't leaving to visit family had been invited. Squire and Kelly would be home for the holidays soon, and Chelsea was looking forward to filling the homestead with people again.

Her family had a tradition of exchanging gifts during the Christmas Eve feast—which Kelly had helped Chelsea plan. Now Chelsea needed the perfect gifts for her family, friends, and cowhands.

She ducked into the hardware store, where she'd surely find something a hardworking cowboy could use. The smell of buttery popcorn hit her like a raging bull. She took a deep drag of the scent that sent her right back to her childhood. She used to love coming to town with her dad just so she could get a free bag of popcorn.

"Afternoon, sugar," the checker said as Chelsea approached. "Popcorn?"

"Yes, ma'am."

Bonnie turned, her once dark hair salted with gray. "How's your momma, honey?"

"She's great." Chelsea accepted the bag of popcorn. "You still working here, Bonnie?"

The woman laughed. "I think they'll bury me out back."

Chelsea smiled, lifted her popcorn in farewell, and started scouting the aisles for gifts. Apparently, lots of other people had had the same idea, because the shelves seemed a little bare. Garth and Tom didn't need sprinkler heads or pipe fittings.

She turned down the next aisle, and her heart lightened at the rows of gloves before her. She crunched through a handful of popcorn as she searched for just the right pair.

THANK *you for your patronage to Courage Reins! We will happily accept the grant in the amount of $65,500 and agree to the terms and conditions in the contract provided.*

Chelsea managed to finish the acceptance email and hit send before she folded her arms on the desk and rested her head in them. The tears pressed so close, but she held them back. Her cheeks had been permanently pruny lately, and besides, she had work to do.

Kelly and Squire would be arriving later that afternoon, and Chelsea was determined to have his bedroom ready for him and a guest bed made for Kelly in the basement. She needed to vacuum, marinate the steaks, and hang the last holiday decoration: Her mother's pine wreath for the front door.

She worked at a feverish pace—the only way she could keep her mind from wandering to Pete and the house that loomed three hundred yards from her front door.

Her cooking lessons had been going well, and she could boil pasta now. She made herself a pot of spaghetti without any incident, and she wanted to text Pete and tell him the news. She wanted to take him the leftovers and witness his smile when he told her, "Good job, sweetheart." She wanted to feel his arms around her and his lips against hers.

Instead, she set out the bowls and texted Tom that the boys could come eat if they wanted to. The garlic bread was store bought, but she had to start somewhere.

Chelsea pulled out the roll of wrapping paper she'd bought and wrapped the new leather gloves she'd purchased for each of the cowhands, Tom, and Garth. She wrapped and tied bows around candy bars for each of the patients at Courage Reins, as well as Brett.

For Pete, she'd created and designed the Courage Reins website, complete with a year of hosting, with the PATH International badge, a sponsors page, services, pricing—which she still needed to confirm with him, if only they were on speaking terms—and construction photos of the property.

She could've emailed the web address to him, but selfishly, she wanted to be present when he saw it. She imagined the way his eyes would light up, the slow curve of those delicious lips, the wonder and amazement with which he'd look at her.

Then heat would crowd the admiration in his eyes, and he'd kiss her, hold her, love her the way he used to.

Icicles stabbed her lungs, barbs of cold pain that forced her to double over, searching for breath.

The episode passed quickly; she cleaned up after the cowhand's spaghetti lunch and wrapped herself in a thick quilt as she moved to the front porch to wait for Kelly and Squire.

Pete's house had gone up quickly, especially after he was forced to leave his cabin. She knew he was sleeping in the unfinished structure, as the tent had disappeared from his backyard. He had no heat or electricity, but anything was better than being subjected to the range winds in December.

He'd ordered a beautiful, decorative front door with tall panes of blue glass. She remembered the one time she'd told him she used to dream of a door like that. She wondered what other marvels she'd find behind that door, and if she'd ever be able to see them. The thought of never stepping foot in the house he'd designed and built brought a pythonic squeeze behind her eyes. A slow headache started, and she tore her gaze from Pete's house.

Her phone chirped out that she had an email, and she swiped to open it. Her smile stuck, turning emotional as she read Ms. Reyes's testimonial for the website. She'd sent a picture of Mari riding Peony, and the sob Chelsea had been containing for hours crashed through her defenses.

Ms. Reyes's testimonial was the last one Chelsea needed for the site, and she thumbed out a quick thank you message with tears leaking down her face.

* * *

"So you're not together?" Squire's confusion was cute, really. At least at any other time it would've been. Chelsea couldn't explain it, didn't have the words to describe what had happened.

"No," she said. "It's complicated."

Kelly put her hand on Squire's arm. "It always is, isn't it?"

"Did he hurt you?" Squire asked. "Because I'll march right over there—"

"Of course he hurt me," Chelsea said. "Look at me." She pushed her mashed potatoes—which she had made by herself, thank you very much—around her plate, her appetite back to nothing since Pete's departure from her life.

"He promised me he wouldn't hurt you." Squire reached for his cowboy hat, like he'd be leaving now.

"He's made a lot of promises," Chelsea said. "He's trying to keep them all." She exchanged a glance with Kelly, pleading for her to influence Squire to stay.

"Squire," she said. "Why don't you go show Finn the horses? He's been begging to see them since we left College Station."

"Horses!" The little boy shot from his seat, his cowboy boots tapping against the tile as he flew toward the door. "Come on, Squire."

Squire gave Kelly a knowing look and Chelsea a pitied one before he crammed his hat on his head and followed Finn. "My friend Pete owns the horses now, so we'll...."

Chelsea lost their voices as they moved down the stairs. She laid her head in her hands and moaned. "What am I going to do?"

"I have an idea," Kelly said, cleaning up the dinner dishes. "But you won't like it."

"Do I look like I like anything right now?" Chelsea forced herself to stand and help. "I always make up a box for Brett."

Kelly scooped a slice of chicken and a dollop of mashed potatoes into a Tupperware. "I'll take it down to him."

"He hasn't come back from Pete's yet."

"Oh, so you spy on the place."

Chelsea chuckled, a sound that morphed into a sob. "All day long. I'm pathetic. I mean, he chose his program over me. Said it right to my face. Why can't I let him go?"

"Love has deep hooks," Kelly said.

"Sharp too."

"He'll come around. Most men do. But, you can encourage him to come around a little faster. I mean, if you want." She busied herself with scrubbing down the counter, which suddenly needed to meet health code requirements.

"How do I do that?"

"Get him over here for Christmas Eve dinner," Kelly said like she'd been holding it in for the entire eight-hour drive from College Station. "Squire and I will work on him."

"I don't want Squire working on him."

Kelly smiled, her cheeks reddening. "Yeah, you probably do. The man's a romantic at heart."

"Ew, too much information," Chelsea said.

Kelly laughed as she drew Chelsea into a hug. "Here's how it's going to go. Tomorrow, we're going to bake the most delicious pie on the planet. You're going to wear your cutest clothes with lots of perfume and swish yourself over there with the pie. You're going to be *nice*, and you're going to invite him to dinner on Christmas Eve."

"He'll say no."

"Use the holiday. He won't want to be alone on Christmas. Trust me." She flounced over to the couch. "Season of giving and charity and love and all that." When she glanced at Chelsea again, Kelly's eyes held a predatory glint. "And then you're going to let me ask him a few questions."

Hope ballooned in Chelsea's chest though she wished it wouldn't. Balloons popped, and the sound startled her, scared her, scarred her.

"Good morning." Chelsea held the pie pan with a death grip, sure she was going to drop it any second.

Pete blinked at her, one hand still on the doorknob inside the house, the other holding a hammer at his side.

He wore his tank top while he worked, and Chelsea focused on his scars.

"I wanted to bring you a little sampling of what you'll get at dinner tomorrow night. If you'll come, that is. It's Christmas Eve."

He stared at her, and she was glad Kelly had made her wear the black leggings with the knee-high boots. The black and white blouse she wore flowed around her curves without giving away too much. He took a deep breath, his eyes closing for just a moment.

Extra perfume as a weapon against his defenses—check.

"There will be a lot of people there," she said. "Squire and Kelly and Finn arrived yesterday. Garth is coming. Brett too. Tom is staying on the ranch for Christmas. My parents." Her voice stalled at the emotion raging in Pete's eyes.

"It's pecan." She thrust the pie toward him and he took it. "I made it myself."

That finally snapped him out of his silence. "You made this yourself?"

"Fine, Kelly helped." She cocked her hip. "And we only had to call my mom once. But look at it. Isn't it gorgeous?" Pride swelled in Chelsea's chest. If she'd known how satisfying cooking something delicious could be, she might have learned earlier.

"It sure is."

In the past, he'd have tacked "sweetheart" onto the

end of that sentence. She missed the endearment so much a wave of disappointment rolled over her shoulders.

She met his gaze to find him staring at her, the pie already forgotten. A blush crept up her neck. "So will you come tomorrow night?"

"Chelsea—"

"Please don't say no," she said, resorting to begging though she'd promised Kelly she wouldn't. "I really want you to come. There will be a lot of people there. You won't even have to talk to me. It's Christmas Eve, Pete. You shouldn't be here alone, without heat or electricity."

He looked at the pie again, then lifted his eyes to hers. "How much are you cookin'?"

"I make a mean mashed potato now, I'll have you know." She smiled, sensing a victory. "But my mom is doing all the baking, and Kelly is making ham and creamed corn."

"I do like creamed corn...."

PETE WATCHED Chelsea sashay back to her homestead, that blasted black and white blouse blowing in the wind. He'd wanted to take the pie, fling it over his shoulder, and take her into his arms. He wanted to tell her that the only person he longed to talk to was her. Only her. Always her.

Every nerve in him still stood at attention, and the woman had left ten minutes ago.

He'd expected Squire to come over last night, but the Major had stayed away. He knew he couldn't avoid him forever, so when he walked into the house like he owned it that afternoon, Pete wasn't surprised.

"Major." Pete wiped his hands on a paint rag and shook Squire's hand. "How was the drive?"

"Good, good." Squire scrutinized the house, skimming the gray paint with white trim and running his fingers along the dark granite countertops Brett had installed that morning. "This is almost done."

"Water'll be on next week. Electricity the week after that. Then I'm movin' in."

Squire grunted. "Kelly and I are living off noodles and canned meat."

Pete laughed. "I got a pretty big loan for all this," he said. "How is Kelly? Finn?"

"Amazing." Squire pinned Pete with a look the Lieutenant knew all too well.

"Lay it on me."

"What happened with Chelsea?"

"I fell in love with her." Pete raised his chin, not to make it a better target for Squire but to show he wasn't afraid of the truth. "But I have nothing to offer her. She wanted me to live in *her* house, use *her* money to pay bills, eat *her* food." Pete shook his head. "I couldn't do it."

Squire's blue eyes softened. "You've always wanted to make your own way in the world."

"I promised my momma I would."

"You promised me you wouldn't hurt my sister."

"I'm trying to do both."

"This place is almost done."

"Almost."

"Looks very much like a house Chelsea would like."

"I did design it with her in mind."

"So you're going to get back together with her."

Pete sighed, wishing his frustration and irritation could go with the exhalation. "There's a long way to go before I can support a family with Courage Reins."

Squire considered him, his narrowed eyes and flat mouth making Pete uncomfortable.

"It's a long way to go alone," he finally said.

* * *

PETE'S STEPS slowed as he ascended the staircase to the deck and those French doors he'd entered so many times before. The wall of windows that allowed him a glimpse into the kitchen showed that he was one of the last to arrive, just as he'd planned.

He'd driven to town and purchased two gallons of vanilla ice cream to go with the Christmas pies he hoped Heidi had made. Squire had bragged about his mother's Christmas baking for months in Kandahar. Pete wanted first-hand experience, with ice cream.

He entered the house to a wall of noise and light and happiness. The homestead was alive again, with people and food in this kitchen. Chelsea was doing what she said she would, and a surge of joy for her spilled from his heart. She'd come so far in only a few months.

"Pete!" Heidi wrapped him in a tight embrace. "It's so good to see you. The house is looking grand."

"Thanks, Heidi. I brought ice cream."

"Oh, ask Chelsea where she wants that. I think she bought two bags of ice, so the freezer in here might be full."

Heidi had obviously not gotten the memo about him and Chelsea. But he maneuvered through the crowd, saying hello and smiling and avoiding shaking hands because of the ice cream he carried.

"Ice cream?" he asked Chelsea, who stood at the stove stirring the creamed corn. "Your mom said to ask you where to put it."

She wiped her bangs out of her face with the back of her hand. "Uh." She drank him in, the happiness at seeing him evident in her eyes and the curling of her mouth. "You came."

"I said I would."

"I still wasn't sure."

With the crowd in the kitchen, snacking on crackers and a cheese ball on the counter, their conversation went unnoticed.

"Where should I put this?" Pete's feet felt like moving, and moving fast. He couldn't be here, in this happy-happy family space, and not take Chelsea's hand. He ached to have that reality, and impatience surged through him. "It's melting."

"Out in the garage," she said.

He marched away from her, relishing in the iciness of the cartons against his fingers. Physical pain didn't hurt nearly as much as the idea of eating Christmas Eve dinner with Chelsea and not holding her close while they sang carols. Of going back to his dark, heatless house alone, kissless and without the promise of seeing her smile on Christmas morning.

After he'd stowed the ice cream in the freezer, he leaned his forehead against the refrigerator door. "I can't do this," he said. Pete didn't take unnecessary risks with his life, not since Kandahar. Why was he risking his heart for a woman he couldn't have?

"You better get back in here," Squire said from the doorway. "Kelly sent me out here to make sure you don't skip out on Chelsea. On all of us."

"I don't know if I can go back in there, Major." Pete sat down on the bottom step, the concrete cold through his jeans. Didn't matter. The only thing that mattered was finishing his house and making Courage Reins profitable. Then he could consider adding Chelsea to the mix.

Squire settled next to him. "I told Chelsea this would be hard for you. That you didn't like crowds, and that wasn't really an incentive to come."

"I came because she asked me to."

"You came because you're in love with her. And when the woman you love asks you to do something, you do it."

"It hurts to see her. She's already surrounded by people she loves." Pete swallowed hard, glad beyond measure that Chelsea had friends and family that loved her and supported her, overjoyed that the home she'd wanted to create had been achieved. "I don't need to be here. *I'm* the one hurting her."

"If you leave, she'll go ballistic," Squire said. "I believe that was the word Kelly used. The mania in my sister's eyes wasn't hard to miss, I know that."

"Squire!" Kelly poked her head into the garage. "There you are. I need you to slice the ham."

"Comin'." He stood and put his hand on Pete's shoulder. "I can't order you to get back in there, but I hope you'll come anyway." He trudged up the stairs and into the house, leaving Pete to his thoughts.

Laughter and chatter filtered to his ears, a droning noise that spoke of love and camaraderie. All of her friends and family were his too. Heidi would be disappointed if he left. Brett, Garth, Tom, Squire. All of them.

He rejoined the group, sticking to the corner of the room so he could watch. Frank pinched off a piece of bread when Heidi wasn't looking, and Finn did the same. The two quietly celebrated together that they'd fooled her, which made Pete smile and remember his own momma who used to swat his hand with a wooden spoon when he tried to sneak a taste of their Christmas cake.

Kelly spotted him and said, "Pete, come help set the table."

"Yes, ma'am." He copied her placement of plates, knives, and napkins as she created place settings at two folding tables that had been pushed together into one wide platform so they could all sit together.

"I have cards here," she said. "You can decide where people sit." She leaned closer. "But I want to be next to Squire." She squeezed his bicep and smiled before she hurried over to the stove, where Chelsea looked a little panicked.

Pete put Frank and Heidi next to each other. Finn next to Frank, then Kelly and Squire. He felt safest next to the Major, so he put himself there. His natural instinct was to put Chelsea next to him, and the other three men along the other side of the table.

He glanced up and found Kelly watching him though it was obvious she was trying real hard not to. Squire didn't even try to hide the fact that he was staring, his eyebrows raised. Heidi had paused in the cutting of rolls, her attention on him as well.

The kitchen quieted and activity ceased, that same moment of stillness and peace Pete had experienced previously descending on him.

He placed Chelsea's name card next to his and continued around the table, noting Squire's approval and Kelly's wide smile.

Dinner preparations ended, and Frank said grace, his

voice catching when he expressed gratitude for the people in the room and the bounty of friendships and food they enjoyed. Pete's eyes teared, not because of the prayer, but because his own heart swelled with gratitude for all that had happened this year.

He'd spent last Christmas alone, in an Army hospital ward in Virginia. The holiday at Three Rivers didn't compare to any previous celebration Pete had experienced, even with his momma and granddad.

"Amen," he said with the others, doing his best to be present for the meal. He succeeded in laughing and talking, but it felt forced, acted out.

"So, Pete," Kelly said as Chelsea got up to brew coffee. "Tell us about Courage Reins. We know little about it." She held Squire's hand on top of the table and gave him a smile.

"It's comin' along," he said, well aware that Chelsea could hear every word. "I've lined up a psychologist and the construction is going smoothly. I'm hoping to recruit volunteers in the new year, get a full-time office manager, and set up a website."

"I thought Chelsea was helping." Kelly gave Chelsea an obviously fake look of confusion. "Aren't you his office manager?"

"Kelly." Chelsea shook her head and studied her hands in her lap.

Silence settled on the group, until Heidi announced, "Time for the gift exchange."

Pete's insides iced. He leaned over to Squire, the frost inside cracking with the movement. "Can I go now? I don't have gifts. I didn't know I was supposed—"

"You go now, and you die," Squire whispered. "At least that's the message I'm getting from this death grip Kelly has on my hand." He lifted their twined fingers an inch off the table. Kelly shot Pete a look that said, *Stay put, Mister.*

Which meant Chelsea had something planned. A kernel of anger popped inside him, more and more exploding as the heat rose through his body. Did she want to embarrass him?

Heidi started first by passing out packages to everyone at the table. Tom and Garth got all-in-one tools—"A rancher's best friend," Frank claimed. Brett got a new tool belt that was ten times nicer than the one Pete had seen him wearing, and Pete received a new coffeemaker.

"For your new house," Heidi said. "Of course, I expect to be invited to the housewarming party. Maybe I'll get you something for that too." She beamed at him, her admiration of him evident.

"Thank you, ma'am." He nodded at her and Frank, the image of his momma and granddad too overwhelming to say much more. Heidi felt like a mother to him, saying and doing what his own momma would've said and done.

Squire and Kelly passed out gifts, and thankfully, Tom, Garth, nor Brett had anything for anyone. Pete announced he didn't either, and looked at Chelsea, who'd been sitting next to him, her fingers wrapped around her coffee mug like they were freezing.

"I guess it's my turn." She passed out leather gloves and chocolate to the other boys, but Pete got an envelope. He turned it over to open it, but she covered it with her fingers. "Later, please."

He slid the envelope under his dinner plate, his curiosity spiking up to the clouds. While Heidi got up to serve dessert, Chelsea poured more coffee and Kelly turned on Christmas carols. Pete determined not to open the envelope until morning, when it was truly Christmas.

Half an hour later, thoroughly stuffed full of three slices of Heidi's delicious pies—all the things Squire had bragged about were true—and all the conversation he could handle, he seized onto Garth's goodnight and followed him out. "You sleepin' on my couch?" the foreman asked as they crossed the lawn.

"Nah," Pete said. "The house isn't that cold, and I have lanterns."

"You're always welcome," Garth said, heading down the path toward the foreman's cabin.

"Thanks," Pete called after him, the envelope like a brick in his back pocket. He took his time walking the distance to his house, taking seconds to finger the door he'd ordered for Chelsea and linger in the bathroom where he'd installed a clawfoot tub last night.

He sighed as he sank onto his Army cot, her envelope

pinched between his fingers. He tucked it under the sheet and closed his eyes.

His dreams weren't filled with fire and gun pops and screaming. They held a whole new form of torture as he thrashed with visions of Chelsea standing at the stove in the house he'd built for her, feeding chickens in the yard he'd planted for her, holding hands with a small girl who looked just like her, except with Pete's green eyes.

Chapter Seventeen

Chelsea closed her eyes and grinned as the Christmas bells rang at the church. Nestled between Kelly and Squire and her parents, she wept. Wept with gratitude for being here in Three Rivers, where she'd been able to heal from deep wounds she'd thought would never scab over.

She hadn't heard from Pete last night after he'd left. She wondered if he'd opened her envelope. Wondered what he thought. Wondered if she'd see him at church this sacred morning.

Finn said something too loud, and Squire collected the boy onto his lap to shush him. The horses had taught her how to be more observant, how to feel subtle shifts in movement or mood. She'd gotten very good at adjusting her riding position to the needs of the horses, and now she sensed the pure love Kelly had for her brother.

Chelsea's mind ached. A deep ache that went on and on, through days and weeks and months and years. She thought she knew pain when Danny had died, but this level of emotional turmoil didn't even exist on a scale somewhere.

She took a deep breath as the last bell faded into silence and the pastor stood to take his place at the pulpit. She held the air, then released it. Peace filled her, and the last fissure in her heart evaporated.

"Faith begins with a single step," Pastor Scott said, a statement with which Chelsea agreed. She'd taken a single step to come home. A single step at a time with Pete.

As the pastor continued to speak about faith, and hope, and patience, Chelsea's tumbling thoughts righted themselves. This was just another step in her relationship with Pete. Maybe a misstep, but not something to divert her to another path completely.

He hadn't chosen Courage Reins *over* her. He'd chosen Courage Reins *because* of her. She wanted to smack herself in the forehead, trip over everyone to get out of the pew, and call Pete right now.

Her right leg began to bounce and bounce and bounce. Her mother finally put her hand on Chelsea's knee. "What's the matter, dear?"

"I need to talk to Pete."

"I saw him come in right as the bells started," her mother whispered. "Talk to him after."

Impatience rumbled through her mind, jumbled her thoughts again, bumbled the words she needed to get out.

* * *

PETE DELIBERATELY ARRIVED LATE to church, sneaking in just as the Christmas bells started. He'd charged his phone in his truck the entire way from the ranch, hoping he'd have a strong enough signal to pull up Chelsea's Christmas present.

Inside the envelope, she'd placed an index card. On it, she'd scrawled one line of text. A website address. A website address for Courage Reins.

Without power and without a computer, Pete hadn't been able to look at it before heading to church.

Now, as the bells rang out wildly, celebrating the birth of the Savior, Pete found his own savior right here on earth.

The Courage Reins website was flawless, with beautiful graphics done in blue and brown. Tabs for services and pricing flowed seamlessly into a tab titled testimonials and then sponsors. He tapped there, surprised to find a half dozen icons.

Six sponsors. He only knew of the one she'd secured and the rubber stamp company in Utah—which he hadn't told her about and so wasn't on the website.

A precious gift she'd given him. The amount of work it

must have taken her to find those sponsors, research them, send applications, manage responses.

He glanced up, staring a hole in the back of her head. *Please turn*, he thought. *Please come talk to me.*

Her shoulders began to bounce, but she didn't get up and move.

He hadn't heard a word of the pastor's sermon, his own personal revelation much stronger at the moment.

The sidebar showed the PATH International badge. They must've been accepted into the organization.

Another blessing.

She was his blessing. How could he have ever thought he could survive without her? Why hadn't he seen that she was as invested in Courage Reins as he was?

"Chelsea," he whispered.

She didn't move; the slight vibrations rippling through her hair went out as Heidi leaned over and whispered something to her.

He clicked on the testimonial tab, unprepared for what he'd find.

Glowing paragraphs with accompanying photos from Reese, Ms. Reyes, Squire, and—his breath caught as he looked into those midnight blue eyes he loved so much. He reached out and touched Chelsea's face, as if she could feel his gratitude and love through the device.

Her testimonial about Courage Reins broke him in seconds.

I didn't think I needed therapy. I haven't been overseas.

I don't have a mental disability or physical injuries that won't heal. But my heart was broken. I had emotional scarring no one could see—except my horse partners, Peony, Baywatch, and Hank. And the director of Courage Reins, Peter Marshall.

He knew I needed help, and though I tried to resist him —and the charms of the horses—in the end, they healed me. I can't say enough good about the equine riding program. Even if you think you're fine, come see what the horses at Courage Reins can do for you.

His heart thudded with rivers of emotion. Anxiety, restlessness, love. He bolted to his feet and strode up the aisle. He didn't care that he was causing a disturbance. He needed to speak with Chelsea *now*.

"Excuse me, sorry," he said as he pushed down her row. "Sorry, ma'am. Excuse me. Slide over, Squire." The Major made room for Pete, who wedged himself between Kelly and Chelsea, his arm around her shoulder.

"What are you doing?" she hissed as several older ladies turned to peer at them.

"I opened your envelope, sweetheart."

She started to cry, and Pete's chest pulsed in and out with his sudden rapid breathing. She pinched the bridge of her nose and buried her face in his chest. He held her, his own tears dripping into her hair.

"Can we go now?" he asked.

She nodded and stood up and together they tripped down the row and out of the chapel. She kept right on going until she escaped the church altogether, her shoulders heaving with sobs and her high heels buckling as she lost her balance.

Pete caught her. "I got you," he said. "And I don't want to ever let you go again." He pressed his face into the crook of her neck. "I'm so sorry, sweetheart. I'm so sorry."

Chapter Eighteen

Chelsea's emotions spiraled, first up and then down. All she'd wanted for weeks was Pete to call her sweetheart, for Pete to talk to her, for Pete to hold her like he was now.

Why then, did she feel like she was about to be sick?

"Did you like the website?"

"Like it?" Pete anchored one hand on the small of her back, the other lilting through her hair. "I love it. I love you."

She smiled against Pete's heartbeat, which thumped along steady and strong. He hummed a lullaby in her ear, and everything in the atmosphere aligned.

"You wanna go see your Christmas present?" he asked.

"You got me something?"

"Sweetheart, I've been workin' on it for over a month."

He stepped back, a shy grin on his face, and enveloped her hand in his. "We can go after church if you'd rather go back in."

A new jittery pitter rose in her chest. Anticipation.

"No, let's go see my present."

Pete drove his truck out to the ranch, one hand on Chelsea's and one on the wheel. "It's out here?"

"You've been lookin' at it for weeks," he said.

"The house." She spoke with awe, with suspicion, with doubt.

"It's for you," he said. "Every color choice, every detail I picked out. I thought of you livin' there with me, what you'd like." He refused to look at her, like the empty road needed his utmost attention.

She adored the flush rising up his neck. She adored his nervous swallow. "I adore you," she said.

"I hope you like the house too." He glanced at her, and she saw the fear there, the desire for her to like what he'd done for her.

They pulled into the driveway, and then the garage. "Extra wide," he said. "So both cars fit, and we can put bicycles over there, and strollers, and—" He cut off like someone had pressed mute on his vocal cords. "I mean, I don't know if you want kids. I want kids." He peered at her, his blushed face and green eyes the perfect decoration for Christmas. "Do you want kids, Chelsea?"

"What if I didn't?"

A cloud darted across his eyes. "Well, we'd have the horses. They're like big babies."

She threw her head back and laughed before leaping into his arms. He caught her around the waist, his smile growing. "You teasin' me?"

The moment sobered, and Chelsea leaned her forehead against Pete's. "I only want kids if they're yours."

He kissed her, the embrace quickly turning passionate. Just as fast, he pulled back. "Okay, then." He cleared his throat. "We have way more house to see, so let's hold that thought."

He led her into the house, which opened on her right into a huge family room, where that blue glass door welcomed everyone.

"The dining table will go here," he said, gesturing to the large space in front of them. "Extra-long bar. I know how you like to eat breakfast at the bar."

On the left sat a gourmet kitchen, with granite counter tops and white cabinets. A dark hardwood ran throughout the space. She released his hand and trailed her fingers along the dishwasher, the stove built into the island, the back door that led to a patio.

"Pete." Her voice choked, and happy tears filled her eyes. "This is wonderful."

"You're wonderful," he said. "That testimonial...." He looked away this time, his tone too high to be normal.

"I only wrote the truth," she said.

He nodded, blinking fast. "I saw the sponsors page too. You've got a lot to tell me."

She smiled, imagining next Christmas with him in this house. Her heart doubled and tripled like rising bread dough, until it felt close to bursting. "After we see the house," she said.

Six Months Later

Pete paced in his bedroom, the old-fashioned ring box taunting him from the dresser. Someone knocked, and he nearly jumped out of his boots.

"Get in here," he hissed to Squire, who stood grinning on the other side of the door. Pete ran his hand through his hair as he glanced down the hall to make sure Chelsea wasn't there. He didn't know why she would be. He was the one planning all the surprises.

"You're as jumpy as a wet cat," Squire said. "Relax."

"Easy for you to say," Pete grumbled. "You asked Kelly to marry you already."

"Chelsea's gonna say yes."

"It's not that part I'm worried about."

Squire looked at him, really peered through Pete's nerves and pacing. "Then what's the problem?"

Pet released a heavy sigh. "I don't know."

"She won't care if Brett lives here. He's been livin' in her basement for months."

"Right," Pete said. Once they'd finished the house, Pete and Brett had moved in. Chelsea had volunteered her furniture, which was in storage in Dallas. She and Pete had rented a truck and made the two-day trip in twenty-four hours because she didn't want to see anyone she knew in the city.

Pete suspected she hadn't fully healed, but he couldn't wait any longer to propose. Living in this house he built for her without her was the cruelest form of torture he could think of.

"So are you gonna go ask her?" Squire asked. "Because Kelly just texted, and she said Chelsea's rarin' to go shopping."

"Yeah." Pete yanked open the door. "Yes. This is happening." He turned back to Squire, his heart flinging itself against the prison bars of his ribs. "You really think she's gonna say yes?"

Squire laughed and put his hands on Pete's shoulders. "Yes."

Pete sucked in a square breath. "Major, you think I'm the marryin' type?"

Squire dropped his hands, folded them, and backed up. He scanned Pete from the boots to the cowboy hat, his expression thoughtful. "You never talked about settlin' down, Lieutenant."

Pete's mouth went dry. He never had. Never given it

much thought—until Chelsea. Now it seemed getting married was all he thought about.

Squire scanned him, the Army edge in his eyes softening. "But that was when you thought you had nothing to offer a woman but deployments and a new city every few months. You're not career Army anymore, Pete." Squire got real close, his eyes edged with power. "You're not your dad."

Pete swallowed the nerves, the doubts, the fear. "Right." He headed downstairs, where Brett was frying potatoes for dinner. "It's on," he called to his friend.

"You askin' her now?" He flipped off the burner and followed Pete and Squire out of the house, across the road, through the parking lot and into the barn. His facilities were complete, but he wanted to ask Chelsea to marry him in the spot he'd fallen in love with her—and that was in the horse barn, with Peony, Baywatch, and Hank standing guard.

Squire texted Kelly, and not two minutes later, Pete heard feminine voices coming his way.

"But I don't need to see the horses before we go to Amarillo," Chelsea complained.

"Well, I do." Kelly almost yelled her response. "I haven't seen them for so long."

"You've been back for a week."

"Finn loves the horses!"

They came around the corner, and Pete forgot his own

name. He gripped the box in his hand so hard the sharp edges left prints in his palms.

"Calm down, cowboy," Squire said. "It's really not that hard."

The Major had always had twice the confidence of Pete, who'd stopped breathing at the sight of Chelsea walking toward him, her denim shorts and tank top showing more skin than she normally did. Her hair was piled on top of her head, and she was clearly ready for a day at the mall, with makeup and jewelry galore.

"What's going on?" she asked when she saw Pete, Squire, and Brett staring at her. "Kelly?"

Kelly giggled, and the sound snapped Pete into motion. He moved forward, concealing the ring box behind his back. "Hey, Chels."

"Hey." She glanced to her brother, then to Brett. "What's—?"

Pete dropped to one knee, the box darting out so she could see it. "Chelsea, I fell in love with you right here, in front of Peony's stall. You're everything I've ever wanted. Will you marry me?"

She clasped both hands to her chest, which rose and fell in shallow breaths. "Pete." She swallowed and looked at Kelly. Pete couldn't look anywhere but at her. She was going to say yes, wasn't she?

"I—well, I've worn an engagement ring before."

"I know," Pete said, unsure of what else to add.

"Twice, actually."

"Twice?" Pete asked at the same time Squire said, "You've been engaged *twice?*"

"Squire," Kelly admonished. "Shh."

Chelsea puffed out her cheeks and spun away from Pete. "When I was driving here after Danny died, I vowed I'd never wear another engagement ring." She turned back, her eyes glassy and soft at the same time. "I just don't know—"

Pete sprang to his feet and drew close to her. "I don't know who the first guy was," he said. "But he obviously didn't deserve you. I don't know that I do either, but I'll spend every day tryin'."

She looked up at him, her fear turning to trust. She smiled, tears forming in her eyes.

"After all, the third time's the charm, sweetheart." He took the ring out of the box and let the sunlight streaming in the doorway glint off the diamond. "It's my momma's ring. So whaddaya say?"

"Yes," she whispered. "A million times yes."

*** * ***

Want to find out if Squire and Pete's Army buddy Brett can find his happily-ever-after? Keep reading for a sneak peek of FOURTH AND LONG, the next book in the bestselling Three Rivers Ranch Romance™ series today!

Get new free stuff every month, access to live events, special members-only deals, and more when you join the Feel-Good Fiction newsletter. You'll get instant access to the Members Only area on Liz's site, where all the goodies are located, so **<u>join today!</u>**

Sneak Peek! Fourth and Long
Chapter One

The presence of Kate Donnely's son had never been such a burden. Of course, she'd never introduced him to his father before. Sure, she'd thought about what this moment might be like. What she'd say, and how Brett would react. She just never expected to look into the almost black depths of her son's eyes and feel a pinch of resentment, like it was Reid's fault she was currently driving down a dirt road toward Three Rivers Ranch.

It wasn't Reid's fault, that much was certain. The vibrant seven-year-old had been asking about his dad for a few years now. Kate always told him Brett was overseas, being a hero by protecting the country. Not exactly a lie, though Kate didn't know all the details of Brett's service.

She did know he'd left for his deployment to Afghanistan only two months after they'd been married.

She knew she'd found comfort in the charms of another man and asked Brett for a divorce only three weeks into his deployment.

And only a week after that, she found out she was pregnant. That effectively got rid of the other man, but also Brett, whose last email said he'd give her whatever she wanted.

The back of her throat burned as hot as the July sun as she thought of her behavior over the past eight years.

"Time to move on," she muttered. "Find him, tell him, move on."

"What, Mom?" Reid met her eyes in the rear-view mirror.

"Nothing, baby." She painted on a smile to conceal the earthquake shaking her core. "We're almost there."

"And I'll get to ride a horse?"

"Maybe," Kate said. "I haven't been able to talk to my friend." Her voice sounded too low to be hers. Her stomach clenched as tears raged against the back of her eyes.

She turned a corner on the dirt lane and a house came into view. As she neared, she saw another home—this one much newer—to her right, facing the first. As if her insides weren't already rioting against her, now she had another choice to make.

She parked near the older home. "Stay here, okay, baby?" She waited until Reid nodded and then she slipped up the front steps of the first house.

No one answered her constant knocking and repeated doorbell peals. She wiped the sweat from her forehead, cursing the summers in Texas. She thought of California, her destination, and how balmy an ocean breeze would feel about now.

She retraced her steps to the car and drove the few hundred yards to the driveway of the second house. Ranch trucks filled the parking lot in front of the barns to her left, so someone had to be around.

The sound of squawking chickens and a grumbling tractor met Kate's ears when she vacated the car again. No one opened the door at the second house, meaning she'd have to traipse around this ranch until she found Brett.

She almost left right then. Aimed her car west, without a plan of ever returning, of telling him about Reid.

But something pulled at her. Her conscience. God. Something.

Kate knew it wasn't her conscience, and God had long abandoned her. The truth was, she needed the money her mother had left her, but she couldn't have it without telling Brett about Reid.

And he has a right to know about his own son.

Kate opened the driver's door and switched off the ignition. "Come on, baby. We have to go find someone. No one's answering the door."

Reid unbuckled his seatbelt and got out of the car, slipping his trusting hand into Kate's. She squeezed harder than necessary, trying to ground herself for what she was about to do.

She heard voices in one of the barns, so she steered Reid in that direction. "Excuse me?" she called once she'd stepped out of the sun. Her eyes took their sweet time adjusting to the darker interior, but she could make out a man approaching.

She almost bolted, her heart somersaulting through her chest, trying to break free of her ribs.

"Can I help you, ma'am?"

A similar Southern accent to Brett's, but definitely not his voice. How she knew all this time, she wasn't sure. Kate blinked the whiteness from her eyes. "Yes. I'm looking for Brett Murphy? I was told he lives out here."

"Yeah, Brett. He's workin' on the cowboy cabins this afternoon."

Construction. Always construction. A sour taste coated Kate's mouth, though she hadn't been able to blame Brett for his profession. He was a builder when she met him, married him, and sent him off to war. His daddy owned the company, and he was a natural with his hands.

She'd used his job as a wedge between them unfairly, not that he knew that. He didn't know anything.

"Want me to take you back there?" the cowboy asked.

"Just point me in the right direction." The last thing Kate wanted was another witness to her confession.

He turned and pointed through the barn. "Head out

thatta way. Take a right. I think he's down at the foreman's cabin. Biggest one at the end of the row."

Kate thanked him and moved through the barn as quickly as she could. She found the gravel path in front of the cabins easily and slipped around the side of the last one, where she could hear the low drone of a radio playing.

Her sandaled foot slipped in something just as she gained the corner, and life slowed into single frames.

The sight of Brett glancing her way. His eyes widening.

The grip of her fingers tightening on Reid's. His cry of surprise or pain.

The smell of fresh horse dung. Her knee thudding against earth and rocks.

"Kate?" The sound of Brett's voice saying her name made time flow forward again, faster and stronger than before.

She glanced down at her soiled shoe, tears combining with embarrassment so quickly that her face churned like a volcano about to explode.

A dog bounded toward them, a chocolate lab with another little boy right behind him. Kate seized the opportunity to talk to Brett alone, like she'd always planned.

"Reid, baby, why don't you go see if you can play with that boy and his dog?"

Reid gave her a quick glance before running through

the grass toward the dog, who yipped and changed direction toward the other boy.

Kate tried to wipe the offensive substance off her shoe and onto the strip of grass bordering the house, but gave up after the first try. She took a deep breath and pushed it out as she faced Brett.

Another man stood next to him, a tool belt hanging off his hips and sporting a cowboy hat, same as Brett. For a moment, she wasn't sure which one was the cowboy and which one the carpenter.

"Brett, hi." Kate stuck her hands in her shorts pockets. "You look great." And he did. Tall, dark, and handsome, Brett had charmed her from the moment she'd met him. If only she hadn't been so weak, acted so stupidly, kept such a massive secret for so long.

His eyebrows disappeared underneath his hat. "That's what you have to say to me after eight years? 'Hi, Brett, you look great.'?"

"You know her?" The other man spoke so quietly, Kate had to strain to hear him.

"She's my wife," Brett said. "Well, my ex-wife." His gaze wandered to Reid and back to her. "What are you doing here, Kate?"

"Well, about that...." She choked, the words there—always there, planned for years—but stuck stuck stuck.

"What about it?"

"That little boy is your son," she said, her voice

rushing now, the things she'd planned to say abandoning her. "His name is Reid."

Eight years ago:

Dear Brett,

I've written this letter at least a dozen times. I don't know how else to say it, so I guess I'll just say it.

I'm pregnant.

I know you might think the baby isn't yours, but it is. I never—I made mistakes after you left, but that wasn't one of them. Momma is sending me to North Carolina to live with Nana, so when you get back, come find me on the great Magnolia estate in Bryson City.

The baby is due just before Easter, so maybe you can get clearance for a video call that Sunday. Let me know so I can make sure Nana's Internet is paid up.

I'm so sorry about everything. I love you, and I've wanted to erase my last email since the moment I sent it.

I hope you can forgive me, and we can be a family when you get back next summer.

All my love,

Kate

"I'll see you later." Pete, Brett's Army buddy and best friend, walked away. Brett had never seen him move so fast, even while under attack in Afghanistan. Pete disappeared around the side of the cabin, but Brett couldn't hear his footsteps in the gravel.

The words *That little boy is your son* echoed endlessly, drowning everything else out, even that rose-scented perfume Kate always wore.

Her mouth moved, but Brett didn't comprehend anything she said. Her fingers twisted around themselves, and he felt the same sensation tightening his gut, twisting and fisting it until he doubled over.

I have a son.

Brett straightened, the prairie breeze whisking away his ex's declaration. He turned his attention to the dark-haired boy romping through the grass with Finn, Major Ackerman's stepson.

Brett had felt welcome and at home at Three Rivers Ranch with Pete and his wife, Chelsea. He'd been taking care of the homestead, installing new flooring and repainting the interior, one room at a time. He'd been testing his green thumb with some new landscaping this summer and finding himself again after being overseas for so long.

Squire, Chelsea's younger brother, had come home for the Independence Day celebrations and to visit family. Finn had turned seven years old a few days ago, and everyone was attending a big birthday party at Kelly's parents' house the following evening.

Brett had been enjoying his life at Three Rivers: The

occasional construction job, the wide-open range, the hospitality of the people in town. He could do without the constant blind dates the older ladies enjoyed setting up for him, but all in all, he'd been happier in Three Rivers this past eighteen months than anywhere else.

And of course, here was Kate Donnely, ruining it. Brett tore his gaze from his son—*I have a son!*—to look back at the boy's mother. She'd stepped in horse manure, and she looked sweatier than a sinner sittin' in church.

Brett tried not to be happy about those things, but the woman had asked for a divorce—via email—only three weeks into his first deployment. He'd given his permission —what else could he do from half a world away?—and blocked her email address.

She'd never tried to contact him in the seven years since. She'd moved away from Oklahoma City by the time he completed his first tour in Afghanistan. Her parents wouldn't tell him where she'd gone, or give him a forwarding address.

As far as Brett was concerned, Kate Donnely had died.

And yet, she stood in front of him, her hazel eyes wide and scared, her auburn hair curling at the ends because of the heat.

"Do you want to meet him?" She gestured toward the child. "I brought him out here to meet you."

"Where you goin'?"

"California."

Brett crossed his arms, trying to figure out why she'd come now. "You could've just taken him to California. I never would've known." He took a step toward her, which caused her to flinch. A fierce animal roared inside his chest, making his voice scratch his throat as he said, "But now that I know about him, I'm not letting you take him halfway across the country, away from me. He deserves a father."

He stalked closer with every step, anger replacing the shock that had saturated his system.

"Yes, he does," she spat. "And where have you been the past eight years?"

"Right where you left me," he said. "It was obviously pretty easy to find me, Kate. I asked your parents for years where you were. They wouldn't tell me."

Her cheeks turned pink, from rage or embarrassment, he wasn't sure. "I stopped talking to my daddy after Momma died."

Brett felt the weight of her words like another punch to the gut. "I didn't know about your mom." He couldn't bring himself to add his condolences, though a voice whispered that he should be the bigger person and do so.

She shrugged. "I finished nursing school, and I have a job waiting in California." She glanced toward her son. *His* son. "I need a fresh start."

"Seems like you take one of those every few years." Brett wished his words weren't so poisonous, but he couldn't help it. He bit back a hurtful comment, glad to know his self-control wasn't completely gone when faced with Kate.

She started nodding, which caused a single tear to drip onto her cheek. She wiped it away quickly. "My momma told me that you deserved to know about Reid. And I—well, I couldn't leave the Midwest without telling you."

"You could've texted."

She opened her mouth, but no sound came out. Brett suspected there was something more to her little visit, but he couldn't fathom what it could be.

"Or called," he pressed. "Sent an email. You're really good at sending life-changing emails."

"Brett—" Kate's shoulders deflated. "I just wanted you to meet him before we leave."

Cold fear punctured Brett's lungs. He'd never been particularly good with children, but he wasn't about to let Kate know that. She'd robbed him of years with his own son. He turned his fury on her, certain by the way her bottom lip shook that she felt it all the way to her bone marrow.

"I'll let you make the introduction." Brett swept his hand toward the boy, who laughed with Finn like they'd been friends since birth.

"Reid," Kate called as they got closer. "C'mon over here, baby."

She hadn't lost her accent, and something sharp pulled

inside Brett, making his step stutter. He'd always loved the sound of her voice, which had made her email breakup so much more hurtful. He'd lost the timbre of it before the email came, but all the feelings he'd had rushed back with sudden familiarity.

"You chose the name Reid?" he asked, real low so the boy couldn't hear.

"Yes." She drew Reid into her side. "Reid, this is—" Kate glanced at Brett, her eyes wide and watery.

Brett knelt in front of the child, seeing himself in the cut of Reid's jaw, his jet-black hair and coal-colored eyes. No doubt about it, Reid was Brett's son.

He waited for Kate to finish; he certainly wasn't going to make this easier for her.

"This is your daddy, Reid." Kate squeezed the boy's shoulders.

Reid's expression turned from guarded to delighted. "You're back!" He flung his arms around Brett's neck and nearly choked him.

On instinct, Brett wrapped his arms around the little boy and picked him up. Love he'd never known filled his heart, worked its way up his throat, surged all the way to the soles of his feet.

He met Kate's eye over Reid's shoulder. "You're not taking him away from me."

Kate's jaw hardened, and her lips flattened into a stiff line. Brett didn't care. She'd had Reid to herself for years, and Brett suddenly didn't feel like sharing.

Eɪɢʜᴛ ʏᴇᴀʀs ᴀɢᴏ:

Kate,

I've blocked your email address and then unblocked it over and over. You haven't sent me another message, and I can only assume you've gone ahead with the divorce. I won't lie, when I think about it, I feel like someone's ripping out my insides with an icy hand.

I don't understand what happened. We loved each other, and we were happy before I left Oklahoma City. At least I was, because you were my whole world. I don't pretend to know what you went through when I had to leave. I do know I'm awfully lonely out here in the desert, and your messages were all I had.

Sure, my mom's written every week. Even Dad threw in a line in the last letter. But I don't worry about them the way

I do you.

I wish you'd write, sugar. I hope and pray that when the day comes when I get released that you'll be waiting for me at the airport. A man can hope for miracles, right? Out here in the desert, I don't know what else to do.

With love,

Brett

Second Chance Ranch: A Three Rivers Ranch Romance™ (Book 1): After his deployment, injured and discharged Major Squire Ackerman returns to Three Rivers Ranch, wanting to forgive Kelly for ignoring him a decade ago. He'd like to provide the stable life she needs, but with old wounds opening and a ranch on the brink of financial collapse, it will take patience and faith to make their second chance possible.

Third Time's the Charm: A Three Rivers Ranch Romance™ (Book 2): First Lieutenant Peter Marshall has a truckload of debt and no way to provide for a family, but Chelsea helps him see past all the obstacles, all the scars. With so many unknowns, can Pete and Chelsea develop the love, acceptance, and faith needed to find their happily ever after?

Fourth and Long: A Three Rivers Ranch Romance™ (Book 3): Commander Brett Murphy goes to Three Rivers Ranch to find some rest and relaxation with his Army buddies. Having his ex-wife show up with a seven-year-old she claims is his son is anything but the R&R he craves. Kate needs to make amends, and Brett needs to find forgiveness, but are they too late to find their happily ever after?

Fifth Generation Cowboy: A Three Rivers Ranch Romance™ (Book 4): Tom Lovell has watched his friends find their true happiness on Three Rivers Ranch, but everywhere he looks, he only sees friends. Rose Reyes has been bringing her daughter out to the ranch for equine therapy for months, but it doesn't seem to be working. Her challenges with Mari are just as frustrating as ever. Could Tom be exactly what Rose needs? Can he remove his friendship blinders and find love with someone who's been right in front of him all this time?

Sixth Street Love Affair: A Three Rivers Ranch Romance™ (Book 5): After losing his wife a few years back, Garth Ahlstrom thinks he's ready for a second chance at love. But Juliette Thompson has a secret that could destroy their budding relationship. Can they find the strength, patience, and faith to make things work?

The Seventh Sergeant: A Three Rivers Ranch Romance™ (Book 6): Life has finally started to settle down for Sergeant Reese Sanders after his devastating injury overseas. Discharged from the Army and now with a good job at Courage Reins, he's finally found happiness—until a horrific fall puts him right back where he was years ago: Injured and depressed. Carly Watters, Reese's new veteran care coordinator, dislikes small towns almost as much as she loathes cowboys. But she finds herself faced with both when she gets assigned to Reese's case. Do they have the humility and faith to make their relationship more than professional?

Eight Second Ride: A Three Rivers Ranch Romance™ (Book 7): Ethan Greene loves his work at Three Rivers Ranch, but he can't seem to find the right woman to settle down with. When sassy yet vulnerable Brynn Bowman shows up at the ranch to recruit him back to the rodeo circuit, he takes a different approach with the barrel racing champion. His patience and newfound faith pay off when a friendship--and more--starts with Brynn. But she wants out of the rodeo circuit right when Ethan wants to rejoin. Can they find the path God wants them to take and still stay together?

The Ninth Inning: A Three Rivers Ranch Romance™ (Book 8): The Christmas season has never felt like such a burden to boutique owner Andrea Larsen. But with Mama gone and the holidays upon her, Andy finds herself wishing she hadn't been so quick to judge her former boyfriend, cowboy Lawrence Collins. Well, Lawrence hasn't forgotten about Andy either, and he devises a plan to get her out to the ranch so they can reconnect. Do they have the faith and humility to patch things up and start a new relationship?

Ten Days in Town: A Three Rivers Ranch Romance™ (Book 9): Sandy Keller is tired of the dating scene in Three Rivers. Though she owns the pancake house, she's looking for a fresh start, which means an escape from the town where she grew up. When her older brother's best friend, Tad Jorgensen, comes to town for the holidays, it is a balm to his weary soul. A helicopter tour guide who experienced a near-death experience, he's looking to start over too--but in Three Rivers. Can Sandy and Tad navigate their troubles to find the path God wants them to take--and discover true love--in only ten days?

Eleven Year Reunion: A Three Rivers Ranch Romance™ (Book 10): Pastry chef extraordinaire, Grace Lewis has moved to Three Rivers to help Heidi Ackerman open a bakery in Three Rivers. Grace relishes the idea of starting over in a town where no one knows about her failed cupcakery. She doesn't expect to run into her old high school boyfriend, Jonathan Carver. A carpenter working at Three Rivers Ranch, Jon's in town against his will. But with Grace now on the scene, Jon's thinking life in Three Rivers is suddenly looking up. But with her focus on baking and his disdain for small towns, can they make their eleven year reunion stick?

The Twelfth Town: A Three Rivers Ranch Romance™ (Book 11): Newscaster Taryn Tucker has had enough of life on-screen. She's bounced from town to town before arriving in Three Rivers, completely alone and completely anonymous--just the way she now likes it. She takes a job cleaning at Three Rivers Ranch, hoping for a chance to figure out who she is and where God wants her. When she meets happy-go-lucky cowhand Kenny Stockton, she doesn't expect sparks to fly. Kenny's always been "the best friend" for his female friends, but the pull between him and Taryn can't be denied. Will they have the courage and faith necessary to make their opposite worlds mesh?

Lucky Number Thirteen: A Three Rivers Ranch Romance™ (Book 12): Tanner Wolf, a rodeo champion ten times over, is excited to be riding in Three Rivers for the first time since he left his philandering ways and found religion. Seeing his old friends Ethan and Brynn is therapuetic--until a terrible accident lands him in the hospital. With his rodeo career over, Tanner thinks maybe he'll stay in town--and it's not just because his nurse, Summer Hamblin, is the prettiest woman he's ever met. But Summer's the queen of first dates, and as she looks for a way to make a relationship with the transient rodeo star work Summer's not sure she has the fortitude to go on a second date. Can they find love among the tragedy?

The Curse of February Fourteenth: A Three Rivers Ranch Romance™ (Book 13): Cal Hodgkins, cowboy veterinarian at Bowman's Breeds, isn't planning to meet anyone at the masked dance in small-town Three Rivers. He just wants to get his bachelor friends off his back and sit on the sidelines to drink his punch. But when he sees a woman dressed in gorgeous butterfly wings and cowgirl boots with blue stitching, he's smitten. Too bad she runs away from the dance before he can get her name, leaving only her boot behind...

Fifteen Minutes of Fame: A Three Rivers Ranch Romance™ (Book 14): Navy Richards is thirty-five years of tired—tired of dating the same men, working a demanding job, and getting her heart broken over and over again. Her aunt has always spoken highly of the matchmaker in Three Rivers, Texas, so she takes a six-month sabbatical from her high-stress job as a pediatric nurse, hops on a bus, and meets with the matchmaker. Then she meets Gavin Redd. He's handsome, he's hardworking, and he's a cowboy. But is he an Aquarius too? Navy's not making a move until she knows for sure...

Sixteen Steps to Fall in Love: A Three Rivers Ranch Romance™ (Book 15): A chance encounter at a dog park sheds new light on the tall, talented Boone that Nicole can't ignore. As they get to know each other better and start to dig into each other's past, Nicole is the one who wants to run. This time from her growing admiration and attachment to Boone. From her aging parents. From herself.

But Boone feels the attraction between them too, and he decides he's tired of running and ready to make Three Rivers his permanent home. **Can Boone and Nicole use their faith to overcome their differences and find a happily-ever-after together?**

The Sleigh on Seventeenth Street: A Three Rivers Ranch Romance™ (Book 16): A cowboy with skills as an electrician tries a relationship with a down-on-her luck plumber. Can Dylan and Camila make water and electricity play nicely together this Christmas season? Or will they get shocked as they try to make their relationship work?

The First Lady of Three Rivers Ranch: A Three Rivers Ranch Romance™ (Book 17): Heidi Duffin has been dreaming about opening her own bakery since she was thirteen years old. She scrimped and saved for years to afford baking and pastry school in San Francisco. And now she only has one year left before she's a certified pastry chef. Frank Ackerman's father has recently retired, and he's taken over the largest cattle ranch in the Texas Panhandle. A horseman through and through, he's also nearing thirty-one and looking for someone to bring love and joy to a homestead that's been dominated by men for a decade. But when he convinces Heidi to come clean the cowboy cabins, she changes all that. But the siren's call of a bakery is still loud in Heidi's ears, even if she's also seeing a future with Frank. Can she rely on her faith in ways she's never had to before or will their relationship end when summer does?

Second Generation in Three Rivers Romance™ Series

Step back into the heartwarming small Texas town of Three Rivers! This beloved town has captured the hearts of 2.5 million readers and caught the eye of Sony Pictures, and now a new generation of cowboys and cowgirls is ready to take center stage. Scan the QR code below with your phone to check out this new series!

1. The Cowboy Who Came Home - featuring Squire's son, Finn from SECOND CHANCE RANCH!

Seven Sons Ranch in Three Rivers Romance™ Series

Meet the cowboy billionaire brothers at Seven Sons Ranch! Scan the QR code below with your phone to check out this complete series.

1. Rhett's Make-Believe Marriage
2. Tripp's Trivial Tie
3. Liam's Invented I-Do
4. Jeremiah's Bogus Bride
5. Wyatt's Pretend Pledge
6. Skyler's Wanna-Be Wife
7. Micah's Mock Matrimony
8. Gideon's Precious Penny

Shiloh Ridge Ranch in Three Rivers Romance™ Series

Meet the cowboy billionaires in the southern hills outside of Three Rivers! Scan the QR code below with your phone to check out this complete series.

1. The Mechanics of Mistletoe
2. The Horsepower of the Holiday
3. The Construction of Cheer
4. The Secret of Santa
5. The Gift of Gingerbread
6. The Harmony of Holly
7. The Chemistry of Christmas
8. The Delivery of Decor
9. The Blessing of Babies
10. The Networking of the Nativity
11. The Wrangling of the Wreath
12. The Hope of Her Heart

About Liz

Liz Isaacson writes inspirational romance, usually set in Texas, or Wyoming, or anywhere else horses and cowboys exist. She lives in Utah, where she writes full-time, takes her two dogs to the park everyday, and eats a lot of veggies while writing. Find all of her books on her website at feelgoodfictionbooks.com.